We Live in a Jungle

PHIL HEUBACH

Balboa Press books may be ordered through booksellers or by contacting:

Balboa Press
A Division of Hay House
1663 Liberty Drive
Bloomington, IN 47403
www.balboapress.com
1 (877) 407-4847

Printed in the United States of America.

ISBN: 978-1-4525-1669-1 (sc)
ISBN: 978-1-4525-1671-4 (hc)
ISBN: 978-1-4525-1670-7 (e)

Library of Congress Control Number: 2014910403

Balboa Press rev. date: 7/14/2014

Dedication

This story is dedicated to my loving parents, Edith and Edward, for they gave me the will to carry on. Also this story is dedicated to my two young grandchildren, Craig and Katheryn (Kate) for the torch has been passed to them and their generation to help create a better tomorrow.

Chapter 1

At any given time in the heart of somewhere, both near and far, there is a most unusual kingdom known as the Jungle. What makes this land so uncommon is neither the time-etched trees nor the exotic plants, but the unique Animals that live there. And for a few of these Animals, the events yet to unfold will challenge their courage, and eventually alter their concept of life forever.

After another long day, it was time to return home. But first a chosen detour was made as a solitary figure entered the meadow to enjoy the stillness that was there.

Butterflies were fluttering from flower to flower. Green and orange leaves glistened in the late, golden sun as it prepared to set in the fiery sky. With a deep feeling of joy, she gazed over the wonders that came into view.

She breathed in deeply. The sweet fragrance of a thousand flowers was a gift to her keen sense of smell.

Moving deeper into the meadow, she heard the wind singing its favorite song. With her soft, furry paw, she reached out to touch the knee-high grass as it danced with the gentle breeze.

"Nature has its own special beauty," mused the young Rabbit. "May I always remember to take time to enjoy what the Great Spirit has created."

She stopped. Her long ears flicked. She stood perfectly still, now listening for a different sound. Danger could strike at any moment. With a sharp, watchful eye, she searched her surroundings.

Only when she was completely assured that there was no immediate threat, did she turn to recapture the moment, as she watched the setting sun dip below the horizon. The early evening sky put on its display of reds, yellows and blues.

"To see a jungle sunset, what a marvelous way to end another day," she whispered. "One day ending and somewhere far away, a new day begins. Life goes on."

Then, with a sense of sadness, she sighed, "Life goes on, but only for the strong. And for a few who know how to survive."

The sun's afterglow was now completely gone and darkness would soon consume the jungle. The Rabbit gazed about, taking in all that she could, not knowing if she would ever have the opportunity to return.

Such was the harsh reality of living in a land that was ruled by the dictum of tooth and claw. For the weak and defenseless, staying alive was a moment by moment challenge. After another hurried glance, she scampered off leaving the meadowlands for home.

Chapter 2

A new day begins, but only for those who had survived the long night. For this is the Jungle Kingdom where the strong dominate the land. And for the weak, life is a constant struggle.

There was a time, a time forgotten by all but a few, that the Jungle was once a land of peace and tranquility. A vast variety of fruits and greens were abundantly shared by the strong and the weak; the healthy and the sick; the young and the dying.

The old kingdom was a land where sharing was placed deeply in the hearts of every Creature. It was a world where the Lion and the Lamb could lie together in peace, and the Vipers had no need of their poisonous fangs.

The Jungle of their forefathers was a living paradise. Then suddenly, and without warning, in the dark of night, a few of the strongest Creatures became Beast of prey.

So long ago, it is not known who was the first to draw blood, be it the roaring Lion or the speeding Cheetah or the striking Cobra. Those who dared to speculate, believed it was the cold-blooded Alligator of the swamp.

It may never be known who was the first Beast of prey. What is known is that their paradise was lost. And overnight, violence became a way of life.

There was another tragic outcome of their paradise lost. With each passing year, the Beast of prey increased in numbers. Within three generations, they were able to seize dominion over the kingdom. Today, they are known as the Meat Eaters.

The Saber-toothed Tiger was on the prowl. He was hungry and mean, which was nothing new for this jungle Beast. His meanness became so severe, even against his own kind, that the other Tigers banned him from the pack. Over time, they declared him an Outlaw. The hunter became the hunted.

The past three years saw the Tiger become a vicious loaner, devouring anyone who crossed his path. Now old and slow, the Saber's victims were limited to the weak and helpless.

Nearby, a young Creature was making her way through the tall grass. Although sharp of eye, she was deep in thought. In the jungle, more times than not, that could be fatal.

The Saber-toothed Tiger, concealed from view, flicked his pointed ears. "Ah, it's a little Rabbit. He'll do quite nicely for my morning meal."

The Tiger, without making a sound, crouched on his powerful hindquarters, ready to strike. What he lacked in quickness was compensated by his cunning. The unsuspecting Rabbit appeared to be just one more helpless victim to be devoured by one mean, hungry Beast.

With his two long, protruding fangs, the Saber waited. And waited. Now! The Beast leaped with his slashing, sharp claws. But he captured nothing but empty space.

The wide-eyed Rabbit, her ears thumping frantically, was ready to dash off to safety. Still terrified, she hesitated when she realized that her would-be assailant was the outlawed Tiger, now old and dying.

Mortified, the Saber-toothed Tiger growled, "How'd you do that? I planned my leap perfectly."

The young Rabbit flicked her long ears, then stared at the Beast with a confident grin. "What you didn't see was my famous side step. I was quicker than your eye. Right?"

"That you were," groaned the big Cat. "But in my prime, you would have been an easy morsel to entice my hearty appetite. You would have been dead meat."

"That we'll never know," countered the bold Rabbit. "But with my famous jack-rabbit starts, I have my doubts if there was ever a time you could have nabbed me. I'm sooome Rabbit!" Then, with a quick afterthought, she mocked, "From what I've heard, your appetite was well beyond hearty. It was greedy and vicious. But it doesn't really matter, for your saber rattling days are over."

"You're a brazen one, aren't you?" sneered the Tiger.

"I have a lot to be thankful for," replied the self-assured Rabbit.

Unknown to the Rabbit, as she went on boasting about her quickness, the sly, old Saber was thinking of his youth . Unnoticed, he quietly shifted his weight to his powerful hind legs, planning one more mighty leap to snag one arrogant Rabbit.

In mid-sentence, the Rabbit saw the Tiger leap with his outstretched claws. When the wild Beast came down with a heavy thud, he had nothing to show for his mighty effort but a cloud of dust.

This time the Rabbit, more startled than afraid, had sidestepped the slow and awkward Saber with ease.

The Tiger was furious as he turned to a grinning Rabbit. "Did you see my famous side step that time, old brute? Or was I again too fast for your tired eyes?" Her strident laugh added insult to the Tiger's wounded pride.

The enraged Beast glared at his little antagonist. "You're a cocky one, but your days are - - -"

"I've heard that before," interrupted the Rabbit with a defiant flick of her ears. "And from younger and faster Beasts than you, old demon."

The big Cat, his hateful stare still fixed on the little Rabbit, roared his contempt. "I would gladly give up a tasty meal to have the satisfaction of seeing you in a chase with the Cheetah."

For one solid moment, there was fear in the Rabbit's eyes, for no one outruns the Cheetah. The Rabbit shook herself free, then said with a sly grin, "Old demon, from the looks of you, you've had your last meal."

The Tiger swished his tail viciously, but before he could react, he heard the Rabbit assert, "Your fate is there in your eyes, the slow agony of hunger or to be devoured by your own kind. I feel no pity for you."

The Saber lifted up his head and growled, "Conceited imp. You have much to learn about survival. Today was your day. I've been beaten and I'll take your mocking laugh to my grave. But I'm a proud warrior. You could have left me with my pride."

The Rabbit held her head high. Her sharp eyes narrowed their focus on the wild Cat. "You lost your pride long ago when you became greedy and devoured your own kind. You're no warrior. You're a savage, vicious Beast! No matter how painful your death, you deserve whatever you get."

The old Tiger never once stopped glaring at his young tormentor, but he knew his days were numbered. "You miserable scamp, may your death be near and as tragic as mine. That's my *curse* on you."

Then in an effort to regain the spirit of his youth, the embittered Saber-toothed Tiger flexed his muscular shoulders and raised his head high. With a low growl, he turned and disappeared into the brush, leaving the young Rabbit to contemplate her own fate.

Chapter 3

Unknown to the white, furry Rabbit, she was being closely watched. Part of her encounter with the Tiger was seen by a slow moving Reptile hiding low in the tall grass. A scaly foreleg reached out, pushing aside a large leaf to get a closer look.

Then a childlike voice broke the silence. "You sure looked scared when your ears were thumping," said the little Turtle. On his green, spotted face there was a friendly but shy smile, which quickly disappeared when the young Rabbit spun around, her eyes aglow.

With three quick hops, the Rabbit approached the baffled Turtle. She flicked her long ears as she leaned over to confront her smaller antagonist. "I wasn't scared," she protested. "Besides, little one, what do you know of fear?"

Intimidated by the Rabbit's quickness and loud tone, the Turtle stepped back. This only encouraged the Rabbit to move in closer. "I do believe you're nothing more than a bundle of nerves." Then to prove her point, she yelled, "Boo!"

Startled, the Turtle darted into his shell.

The Rabbit was amused. With the Saber-toothed Tiger, she dared to put herself in a life-death situation. Foolish no doubt, but the Rabbit knew her skills. Now, with the little Turtle, she could throw caution aside and have a little fun. In the kingdom, where the Meat Eaters dominated, it was a unique experience for the spunky Rabbit.

Believing that she was in complete control of the situation, the Rabbit contemplated on what to do with her timid, Jungle rival. Bending over, she called out, "Well, little one, I certainly proved my point. And we both know you can't hide in your shell forever. Right?"

There was no reply. But she was not discouraged, knowing that she was sooome Rabbit.

Her next move was to entice the little Turtle to come out of his shell. The Rabbit thought for a moment. It didn't take her long. It never did. "To prove that I mean you no harm," she said pleasantly, "I will show you a few of my skills. Would you like that?"

Again the Rabbit's words were met with silence. "Are you okay in there?" she asked, more curious than concerned.

Not a word was heard. The Rabbit stood up straight and stroked her furry chin. For some unexplained reason, she was now even more determined to impress the Turtle.

"Well, I hope you enjoy the show." Then to herself she said, "Who knows when he sees what I can do, it might help him get over his shyness."

Forgetting herself for the moment, the young Rabbit was on the edge of violating a deep-seated barrier that had been reinforced over three hundred years.

In the Jungle Kingdom, especially for the weak and defenseless, survival was their ultimate challenge. To get involved with another Creature outside your own kind was greatly discouraged on every level. To violate this dictum was considered unwise and extremely dangerous.

"Well, here goes!" called out the Rabbit. With her head held high, she began to scamper about, slow and easy at first. She knew she was good and she wanted to make sure she had the audience of one small Turtle.

"I'm fast and nimble," she shouted loud and clear. "And if you blink, you'll miss the show," she added with a confident laugh.

The Turtle slowly poked out his spotted head. Not knowing if he could trust the Rabbit, he remained cautious.

As easy as the wind blows, the self-assured Rabbit put on a marvelous display of her talents: Jumping over tall bushes, zooming around trees, twirling high in the air, and completing a near perfect backward somersault, landing softly on her feet. Then, without a moment lost, the Rabbit zoomed off with one of her famous jack-rabbit starts.

"Is he ever fast," thought the Turtle, stretching out his neck as far as he dared. "His feet hardly touch the ground."

The Rabbit could see from the corner of her eye that the little Turtle was impressed. So she zipped and zoomed with increasing speeds, becoming nothing more than a white blur. "In a dry, busy meadow," she boasted, "I can run faster than any Zebra and just as fast as the graceful Gazelles!"

The Turtle, a very slow runner himself, was amazed by the bouncing Bunny's speed. His fear forgotten, he emerged from his shell. "Wow! You're really fast!" cheered the Turtle. "You're the fastest moving, highest hopping Rabbit I've ever seen! Boy! You're really terrific!"

That one remark hit a sour note. Without warning, the speeding Rabbit stopped abruptly, whirled around and glared.

"Oh, oh," cringed the bewildered Turtle. "What did I do wrong now?"

Her ears twitching vigorously, the Rabbit stomped over to the Turtle. "Boy did you say? I'm not a boy. I'm a GIRL!"

Before the Rabbit could say another word, the frightened Turtle once again disappeared into his bony shell.

"Don't you try to hide from me in that useless box of yours," warned the Rabbit. Not knowing if she was heard, she raised her voice a little louder. "Do you hear me?!"

Yes he heard. All too well. But too afraid to speak out, the Turtle kept his troubled thoughts to himself. "It might be a useless box to you," he mumbled, "but it's all I have to protect me from the likes of you."

The Rabbit hearing nothing but the whirling wind, was reaching the point of frustration. "Do you hear me?!" she repeated sharply.

The Turtle's ears twitched. But he said not a word, hoping that he would be safe hiding in the darkness of his shell.

"You silly Turtle, you spend so much time in that outdated fortress of yours that you haven't learned how to live. Quit living in the dark ages and grow up!"

The Rabbit paused just long enough to catch her breath. "Come out of that obsolete armored suit and face me!" she demanded. "Right now!" For special effect she punctuated her last words with a hard stomp against the ground.

But the Turtle didn't budge, and a perplexed Rabbit scratched her furry head. "Well, that ploy always worked with my baby brothers," she said to herself. "Now what to do?"

Actually, the Rabbit's temper was more show than real, but that the little Turtle didn't know. And in an effort to escape the Rabbit's apparent anger, he slipped deeper into his hard but cozy shell.

"Come out right now!" she demanded again. "I'm not going to hurt you, just teach you a few lessons on manners."

"No way," thought the Turtle. He was beginning to feel safe where he was. And not knowing what to do, he did nothing. Sometimes, he was learning that was the best thing to do. Nothing.

The impatient Rabbit waited for what seemed to be a long time. With her baby siblings, she was use to having things her own way. And she was in no mood to be outsmarted by a little Turtle. "Do you hear me?!" she called out again. "Answer me!"

Deep in his shell, the Turtle was now feeling quite secure. So, he decided to remain quiet, hoping that the Rabbit would just go- - -a- - - way. "Then I can go home and have something good to eat," he thought to himself.

Still believing she was in control, the Rabbit felt compelled to outwit the little Turtle. "That shouldn't be too difficult for one clever Rabbit," she said to herself. But to do so she would need to come up with a new scheme. It didn't take her long. It never did. Prone to take herself too seriously, she was prepared to go the next step.

Pretending to be fighting mad, the young Rabbit turned on the heat. "Don't you provoke me!" she warned, her blue eyes blazing. "If you don't come out this instant, I'm coming in after you! You're not going to play your silly shell games with me!"

Now the little Turtle didn't wish his home invaded by a foreign Creature. He also knew he couldn't remain in his shell forever. But then, facing this hot-headed Rabbit was something he wasn't prepared to do, either.

He had to think - - - and fast. But fast was not the nature of Turtles, and this little Turtle was slower than most. Even so he tried. But it only added to his confusion.

Under more pleasant circumstances, the Turtle might have realized that there was no way the Rabbit could have gotten her furry body inside his shell. But conditions weren't pleasant, and the slow thinking Turtle could only cope with one thought at a time.

While the Turtle struggled with what to do, the Rabbit was thinking, too. To continue to wait any longer for one silly Turtle would be a waste of her time. "Sometimes, she surmised, " you just can't have it your way." Then with a carefree shrug, "Win some, lose some."

Choosing to call it a day, the Rabbit was prepared to scamper off, when a timid voice was heard from within the shell. "H- - - Here I come," stuttered the Turtle. Slowly he poked out his spotted head, his eyes blinking from the sun.

"Well, it's about time," said the Rabbit, looking very serious. "Now get this straight. I'm a girl and don't you forget it!"

The little Turtle flinched, but he dared not slip back into his shell. "Why me?" he said to himself. "I just wanted to be friends."

"I'm not going to hurt you," said the Rabbit with a firm voice. "That's not my nature. But no one gets away with calling me a boy. Understand?"

"Yes, I understand," the Turtle replied weakly.

"Now hear this! Girls can run, jump, and think just as good as boys. All we need is a chance to be ourselves. Then we would show you and the whole kingdom how much we can do."

The Turtle was overwhelmed. Living at a much slower pace than the fast talking Rabbit, much of what she had said was not even heard. But when he glanced up and saw that look in her eye, he knew more was to come.

The Rabbit leaned over and in a very loud voice proclaimed: "I'M A GIRL AND PROUD OF IT!"

What was loud for the Rabbit was fast and furious for the Turtle. In an effort to avoid the Rabbit's strong words, he jerked backward with so much force that he flipped over onto his back.

Once the shock was over, the Turtle checked to see if he was in one piece. He was. His next thought was to get back on his feet, and as quick as possible. He began to squirm, moving his four legs, his sharp pointed tail, and his spotted head in every direction, all at the same time.

From the young Rabbit's point of view, the squirming Turtle looked completely ridiculous.

But unnoticed by either one of them, with each twisting motion, the little Turtle was slowly slipping deeper into the loose dirt.

As the Turtle squirmed, the Rabbit teased. "If you had more than just the brains you were born with, you would remove that antique armor from your back. That thing you call a shield is nothing more than a trap."

"I wish you would close your trap," said the little Turtle to himself. "Then I could concentrate on getting back on my feet."

But the Rabbit had no thought of stopping. She was just having some fun. "No blood, no pain," she said aloud. "It's the law of the Jungle."

With a glint in her eye, she continued. "You know little one, lugging that heavy weight on your back is like carrying the whole kingdom on your shoulders. No wonder you move with the speed of a rock," she added with a raucous laugh.

Hurt by the Rabbit's cutting remarks, the Turtle now lay motionless. He wanted to speak out, but he said nothing. It was easier to feel sorry for himself than to ask for help.

The Turtle's silence only seemed to encourage the Rabbit to continue her teasing. "It's not every day I find myself with a captured audience for one of my lectures. This must be my lucky day. First the old, vicious Saber. Now a timid Turtle. So, if you want my advice, you'll get rid of that dead weight you call a home and travel free like me."

"My shell might seem useless to you," thought the Turtle, "but I need my shell to protect myself from all kinds of Creatures. But then again, maybe this heavy shell is weighing me down."

Listening to the fast talking Rabbit, the Turtle didn't know what to do. More confused than before, he was now thinking that thinking for himself was not as easy as he had thought.

"I wanna go home," he muttered to himself. "But I'm in serious trouble and unless I get back on my feet, I could be here forever. And forever is a very long time." He was on the brink of asking for help, but old habits are hard to break. And his cry for help remained just a passing thought.

The young Rabbit, still unaware of the seriousness of the Turtle's predicament, appeared both smug and unconcerned. "Well, I guess I'll be off," she said as though talking to herself. "Nothing much happening around here, but a strange looking Turtle basking in the afternoon sun. A waste of time if you ask me."

With those last words pounding in the Turtle's head, the Rabbit sped off. Eventually, she thought, the Turtle would find a way to get back on his feet. With a hop here and a zigzag there, she was out of sight, leaving the Turtle to his own plight.

Now all alone, the little Turtle realized that if he was to get back on his feet, it was entirely up to him. With renewed determination, he started to squirm and twist.

"Oh, oh," gasped the Turtle. "What's happening?" Frantically he looked around to discover that he was beginning to slip deeper into the loose dirt. Afraid to move, he stared at the endless sky above.

"What do I do now?" he squeaked. Desperate, the little Turtle pondered his hopeless dilemma. "If I lie here on my back, any wild Beast might come along and devour me. But if I struggle to get back on my feet, I might be gobbled up by this hole - - - buried alive!"

The Turtle, petrified with fear, lay helpless, his little green eyes blinking with the fading sun.

Chapter 4

The hazy sun was in its downward arc, and the jungle shadows began to lengthen. The free, cool wind softly played its serenade and the rippling waters responded with their own harmonious melodies.

His tiny ears twitched. Another rhythmic sound more threatening than the cool breezes was now heard by the upended Turtle.

The ground trembled. "Oh, oh. It's coming this way," shuddered the Turtle. He could feel the tremors get closer and stronger until the earth shook all around him. Fearful that it might be the hungry Saber, the helpless Turtle struggled to see what it was.

"Well, little one," quipped the teasing voice. "I see you're still in your self-made trap."

The Turtle flinched. It was the Rabbit on her way home before dark. She hadn't been gone long, but to someone in a hole upside down, it seemed like forever. The little Turtle wanted to cry out. He tried, but the words - - - just - - - wouldn't - - - come.

The young Rabbit, however, had no trouble with her words. "You know little one, our problems are always self-made. And those who never learn this will sooner or later find themselves in a *hole* of their own making."

While the Rabbit continued her teasing, the timid Turtle realized he had to do something and fast. Breaking through his silence, a frail voice was heard: "I'm stuck. Will you please help me?"

Before the Turtle could say another word, the Rabbit extended her furry paw. "Sure, all you had to do was ask."

The little Turtle blinked, not believing his own eyes. Afraid to give it a second thought, he reached up.

They touched. Zip! Quicker than a Butterfly's sneeze, the Turtle was up and on his feet.

Unbeknown to the Rabbit and the Turtle, the moment they touched, they had broken generations of conditioning. Both had to struggle through their own inner "demons" before they could make their decision to reach beyond the barrier of isolation. For them, sooner than later, their decision to touch would bring them to a higher awareness. Eventually, their relationship would affect the entire kingdom, bringing a young Rabbit and a little Turtle greater rewards - - - or agonizing failure.

Regardless of their fate, it would be impossible for them to turn back even if they wanted to. For once the mind is raised to a higher consciousness, the mind never returns to its previous level. If the kingdom should survive the Meat Eaters, their touch might someday be known as one of those rare Magic Moments.

"I've never moved so fast," said the Turtle, shaking the dust from his green body. "I feel kind of strange."

"Well, now that you're up and about," replied the Rabbit with a hint of a grin, "you look okay to me."

The little Turtle glanced up. "I just remembered," he said, his voice becoming weaker as he spoke, "I'm still angry with you."

"You don't look or sound angry. When I'm angry the whole kingdom knows it."

The Rabbit's flippant remark caught the Turtle by surprise. He hesitated. Then, surprising himself even more, he gingerly confronted the Rabbit. "You should have helped me when you saw that I was in deep trouble. Stuck in that hole, I could have been - - -"

"Someone's mock turtle soup," she interrupted with a loud laugh.

"What?" said a very befuddled Turtle.

"Just joshing," came her casual reply.

"But why didn't you offer to help me?"

The Rabbit, a full head taller than the little Turtle, peered down her pink nose and replied, "To receive you must first learn to speak up. Why didn't you ask for help?"

Still holding back his anger, the Turtle squeaked, "Why didn't I ask? That's a stupid question."

"Well, then give me a smart answer," she retorted with ease, now feeling in complete control of the situation.

The Turtle's chin dropped. He didn't know what to say. He thought he had a good reason to be angry. Now he wasn't so sure. "I don't know why it took me so long to ask for your help."

"Sure you do," she said, sounding both helpful and condescending at the same time. "I'll give you a moment to think on it, but I haven't got all day."

After a moment or two, the Turtle tilted his head to one side and offered faintly, "Maybe because I was afraid you might have said no."

"I knew I could help you understand," she said with that glint in her eye.

The Turtle looked up and said, this time with a stronger voice. "But you knew I needed help. Any fool could have seen that."

The Rabbit, standing tall, flicked her long ears and stated firmly, "I'm nobody's fool, especially not yours. You didn't catch me in a hole I couldn't get out of. I'm much too clever. And further more, you should never *assume.* It only gets you into trouble. Or into a *hole,*" she added with another loud laugh.

Tired and confused, the Turtle just couldn't take any more teasing. His feelings hurt, tears began to flow.

The Rabbit hesitated, then responded with a tone more pleasant. "Hey, I meant you no harm. And you have no reason to feel hurt. The next time you need help, build up your courage and speak up. Anyone can do that, even you."

"But I'm afraid to," sobbed the Turtle.

"Well, that's your problem," she stated quickly. Then doing the unexpected, she moved in closer and said with a softer voice, "Its okay to cry, if you need to. Maybe I can help you understand that there's nothing to fear. But before we do anything else, let's dry those eyes."

As she brushed away a tear with her soft, furry paw, the Rabbit began what she believed to be another one of her helpful lectures. "It's really a waste of time to be afraid," she said, looking very serious. "Fear doesn't exist. It's only a figment of *your* imagination. Have you ever seen a grain of fear? Of course not. It's only a feeling you get in the pit of your stomach when your head gets in the way." Her last words were concluded with a dramatic sweep through the air with her paw.

The Turtle knew he had much to learn. And he had tried to hear her every word. But he just couldn't think as fast as the Rabbit could talk. And that thing about figment-of-something-or-other really did confuse him. But not to appear completely lost, he kept his troubled thoughts to himself.

The young Rabbit, however, was in her glory. She was in control and that gave her a feeling of importance. Just as satisfying was the thought of helping someone not as smart as she. "This little Turtle really does need me," she said to herself. "I can be his teacher."

Now had the Rabbit been more aware, she might have noticed the empty expression on the Turtle's face. But lost in her own world, she continued. "As long as you choose to hide in your shell, you'll never outgrow your fearful thoughts. Rise above your protective shield and be more like me. Let go and live!"

"That's easy for you to say," sighed the Turtle, again feeling sorry for himself. "I need my shell. You can run like the wind, while I can only creep."

"Nonsense," she countered quickly. "It's not only my terrific speed, you're just creepy." The Rabbit, once again amused by her wit, let loose a strident laugh.

But the little Turtle was not amused. Once more, stung by her teasing, tears filled his eyes.

"Whoops! I did I t again," she said in earnest. "I mean you no harm. Honest. It's just that I talk before I think, er, sometimes. You sure do hurt easy. And you do it so well. Who was your teacher, anyway?"

Not waiting for an answer, the Rabbit swept away another tear. "It's easy to see that you are hard on the outside but soft on the inside. If you want to survive in this uncaring Jungle, you'll have to stop being so sensitive to what others say about you. You need to toughen up."

The Turtle sniffed, trying to hold back his tears.

"Remember," she said softly, "it's okay to cry."

"Well, I don't like being called creepy."

"I didn't mean anything by it," said the Rabbit sounding sincere. "I was just having a little fun."

"At my expense," murmured the Turtle. "That may be fun for you, but not for me."

"I know what you mean," sympathized the Rabbit, but there was that pompous tone in her voice, too. "My five baby brothers call me names. But I've learned to ignore their taunting remarks. Now their teasing doesn't bother me. And if I can do it, so can you. Just don't take me for being a boy. That makes me angry."

"You have *five* brothers?!" asked the Turtle, his eyes now filled with curiosity.

"Yep. And six baby sisters. And like my little brothers, they call me names, too - - - Bossy."

"Wow! *Eleven* baby Bunnies!" blurted the Turtle, his need to cry forgotten. "You sure have a large family!"

"Not really," she replied nonchalantly. "It may seem that way to you being a Turtle, but not to us Rabbits. Who knows, maybe by the time I get home, I might have a few more baby siblings."

"Oh, my," he blushed. "All those Bunnies. And do they call you other names besides bossy?"

"Yep. Sometimes, on one of my *few* bad days, they call me grouchy."

"Grouchy!" repeated the Turtle, who wasn't a bit surprised. "Do they have other names for you?" he asked becoming quite inquisitive.

"Oh, sometimes they call me loud mouth. Then there are days they call me cranky or grumpy."

The Turtle rushed his hands to his mouth in a failed attempt to hold back his giggles. "I'm sorry," he said sincerely. "I didn't mean to laugh."

With her usual serious demeanor, the Rabbit looked directly at the little Turtle. "To be laughed at doesn't bother me. Nor does name calling as I said before. It's called growing up. You should try it sometime. Not only will you feel better about yourself, you might live longer in this senseless kingdom." Then she added, "And yes, I do accept your apology."

"Oh," said a surprised Turtle, who was trying hard to keep up with the fast talking Rabbit. "And thank you for the advice. I do want to grow old."

"Grow up," corrected the Rabbit, slowly shaking her head.

The Turtle nodded. "I understand - - - I think."

"Well, that's a start, little one," she said thoughtfully. For without a doubt, the young Rabbit truly believed she could help the little Turtle. "Why, I can teach him to be more like me," she said to herself.

Feeling both needed and important, the Rabbit was eager to continue. "Do you have any more questions little one?"

The Turtle blinked. He couldn't remember anyone taking the time to ask him a question. Ever. This was fun. "Do you also help your sisters and brothers?"

"I sure do. I do what I can to help my parents with the family chores. My brothers and sisters are pretty neat and I do love them, but there are times when I think it would be great to be an only Bunny. Especially at bath time - - - washing all those looong ears," she added with a dramatic frown.

"*Twenty-two* ears!" he blurted again, his eyes bulging wide. "That's a lot of work for you. But to have all those playmates." The Turtle paused, then pouted, "I have no brothers or sisters to play with. And I get real lonely all by myself. And sometimes - - -"

"Hey! Getting back to names," interrupted the Rabbit, who was more interested in talking than listening. Especially when talking about her favorite subject. "My name is Roberta," she said proudly. "Rapid Roberta. All my friends call me Rapid Roberta because I'm the fastest, zigzaggiest Rabbit in the whole kingdom - - - What's your name?"

The Turtle blinked again almost missing the question. "You sure do talk fast."

"Yes I know," she replied without the slightest effort to slow down, "but that's my nature. Now, for the second time, what's your name?" she said in a hurried but friendly manner.

"They call me - - -" The Turtle stopped, afraid like all the others, she would laugh.

The Rabbit, not knowing what the little Turtle was thinking, again mistook his fear for shyness. She glanced down and smiled encouragement. "Come on. Don't be shy. You can tell me your name."

The Turtle really wanted to be friends with the Rabbit, so he did. But it happened again just as he had feared.

Thump! Thump! Thump! The Rabbit's long ears banged together vigorously as she exclaimed with laughter. "Termite! Your name is Termite?!"

Deeply hurt by the Rabbit's uncaring behavior, the dejected Turtle had only one thought. And that was to get away as fast as he could, which isn't very fast for a slow-footed Turtle.

From the corner of her eye the Rabbit could see the Turtle sneaking away.

Thinking fast, she called out, "Hey! I wasn't laughing at you. I was laughing at the name Termite."

In her voice there was a touch of real concern. This was a good beginning for a young Rabbit who had her own lessons to learn.

Two quick hops and a skip, and the Rabbit was at the Turtle's side. With her paw, she dabbed away a few more tears. "That's no name for a Turtle," she declared. "We can do better than Termite. Of that I have no doubt."

The Turtle let out a deep sigh as one more tear was about to fall. "Do you really want to help me with a new name?"

"Sure do! What's this self-centered jungle coming to if we can't help each other.

The little Turtle hesitated, then said gingerly, "No one has ever offered to help me before."

"Trust me," she asserted. "My word is my promise."

The Turtle sighed again as the Rabbit softly brushed away a falling tear from his cheek. "You must think I'm a sissy for crying," said the Turtle through several sniffles.

"Not at all," she said kindly. "Remember, it's okay to cry."

"Is that a law of the Jungle?"

"No, that's Roberta's law," she stated with pride. "I discovered that all on my own. Actually, the Meat Eaters of this backward kingdom frown on crying. They see it as a sign of weakness. And you know what happens to those who appear weak in this heartless Jungle."

That the Turtle knew, but at the moment he just couldn't remember. Things were moving too quickly for the slow thinking Turtle. He glanced up, tilted his head to one side and said, "I'm trying."

The Rabbit gave a look of encouragement. "It's the first thing we are told by our loving parents before we leave the nest."

"Oh!" eeked the Turtle. "To be weak is to be - - -" He stopped short, not wanting to even think about it.

With a dramatic look in her eye, the Rabbit slowly nodded her head. "So, if we want to stay alive, rather than be someone's meal, we must be clever and appear to be strong."

The Turtle scratched his head. "Then why is crying okay? It would seem to me that - - -"

The fast talking Rabbit interrupted again, assuming she knew what the Turtle was going to say. (The Rabbit seldom followed her own rules.) "In this joyless kingdom you dare cry only with those you trust. Otherwise you're dead meat."

"Oh!" he gasped, as he shuddered all the way down to his pointed tail. Then, quickly as he could, the Turtle changed the subject. "Have you ever cried?"

"Many times little one. Many times."

"Why?"

"Oh, sadness over the loss of loved ones before their time. Which you know happens all too frequently in this bloodthirsty Jungle." After a long pause, she continued with the same soft voice. "Sometimes I cry for the sheer joy of seeing one more sunset. We never know which one will be our last."

The Turtle was moved by what he had just heard. And he liked hearing a softer voice. There were moments, though, that he found the Rabbit's behavior not to his liking. The teasing. But then there were also times when she seemed caring. And sometimes even friendly.

One thing for sure, the Turtle was impressed by the Rabbit's self-confidence. So it felt natural to follow her lead to a shady tree. Together, they sat down on the soft, green grass.

"Now without any further delay, little one, let's find a suitable name for you. Termite will never do."

The Turtle's little eyes gave a look of surprise. "I thought you had forgotten."

"I have a few faults, but forgetting a promise is not one of them."

The Turtle liked hearing that. And to know that he was to have a new name caused chills to run up his back. He turned to the Rabbit and gave her a smile, but she failed to see it. She was too busy thinking.

After a long interval a soft voice broke the silence. "May I help?"

Without changing her demeanor the Rabbit replied, "Of course you can. You learn faster by doing, not watching. And besides it's your name."

So together they worked on finding a new name, with the Turtle rejecting one after the other. A few were no better than the name Termite.

After several more rejections, the Turtle, far from being discouraged, said with a cheerful voice, "This is fun! Thank you for helping me!"

The Rabbit was so deep in thought she didn't respond. With such a long face, she looked very serious. Then, with a belated nod, she said, "We won't quit until you're completely satisfied. I promise."

"All right!" the Turtle cheered again.

Moments passed by, then out of nowhere, "I've got it!" she declared. "How about Timid Turtle for a name?"

"What?" blurted the Turtle, slowly shaking his head. "No, no, no," he added with a very big pout.

"Only kidding," grinned the Rabbit, raising her two paws as though defending herself. "Just kidding. And I do apologize."

Once again the Rabbit was talking much faster than the Turtle could think, but her apology did sound sincere. Although a few doubts remained, the Turtle's pout was gone.

"Now, little one, no more joshing, and we will find a name just for you. That I guarantee."

That the Turtle could say yes to and did, hoping that the Rabbit would just stop - - - her - - - teasing.

Once again, with that serious look on her face, the Rabbit suggested a number of names, and one by one, they were rejected by one hopeful Turtle.

Time past by and behind them the sun was setting low in the western sky. A radiant glow of several shades of reds and yellows were streaking through the clouds.

"Hmmm," reflected the Rabbit. "Tiny. How's that for a name?"

"Tiny," the Turtle whispered. Then, with enthusiasm, he expressed louder, "TINY TURTLE! Yes! I like it." Then softly, "Tiny Turtle. I like the sound of it."

The Rabbit sat up straight, her long ears thumping proudly. "Well, we did it! I knew we could!"

Tiny nodded his spotted head. "I like my new name. Thank you." Then with a childlike smile he said shyly, "Roberta."

"You're welcome," she acknowledged, jumping to her feet. Her movement was so abrupt that Tiny was caught by surprise. Even before he had a chance to respond, he heard Roberta declare triumphantly, "Then so it is! From this day forward your name shall be Tiny Turtle!"

Tiny beamed as he rose to the occasion.

Standing side by side the self-satisfied Roberta flicked her fluffy cottontail. She was quick to believe, without a doubt, that for the second time in one day, she had saved the little Turtle from despair. With her head held high, she proclaimed, "I'm sooome Rabbit!"

She was forgetting, though, that a good part of the Turtle's despair was due to her. "Tiny may the name *I've* chosen bring you and *me* - - -" She stopped and glanced down, and there she saw a very happy Turtle. "Tiny, for a fast thinking Rabbit, in some ways I'm rather slow. At the moment I was only thinking of me. This is your special day."

"I know," he replied with a big smile. "Today I am TINY!"

"And so you are. So let me rephrase my original toast. May your new name bring *you* courage and wisdom. Ah, yes. That should do quite well for a young Tiny who has chosen to learn and grow."

Tiny, feeling a joy all his own, smiled his appreciation. Once again he could feel the chills go up his back. "This is a special day for me."

"May you have many special days," offered Roberta. "And if you wish I'll be your teacher."

Tiny glanced up almost not believing what he had just heard. "I'd like that," he said sincerely."

"I do, too. But I can be demanding," she continued with that determined look on her face. "I'll expect you to pay close attention."

"Oh, I will," Tiny replied eagerly.

"Good. Then you are ready for your first lesson as my pupil." With her soft paws on Tiny's shoulders, Roberta gently turned him around.

An unusual long silence followed. And even though they were standing close together, Tiny was now feeling alone.

"Isn't she beautiful," sighed Roberta.

"What's beautiful?"

"Why the sunset. I can see you have a lot to learn."

"I know I don't know much."

"Well, that's a start," replied Roberta. "But let's try to remember this is your special day, and you don't have to be so hard on yourself. Now just take a good look at our first sunset together. Every night I try to capture the sun before it disappears."

"Where does it go?" asked Tiny naively.

"Little one that's a good question."

Tiny beamed. "I like compliments."

Roberta hesitated, giving Tiny a very long look. Then, resuming her role as the teacher, she went on to say quietly, "Our setting sun goes to begin a new day somewhere in a far off world." (Actually, Roberta really doesn't know this. It was only the Rabbit's habit to impress others.)

Tiny nodded to show that he understood.

"Tiny just gaze at those flaming red colors dancing across the evening sky. It's breathtaking. Without a doubt I would gladly give up a luscious meal to see a glorious sunset."

"I wouldn't," disagreed Tiny with a firm pout. "I like to eat!"

Roberta flicked her long ears and slowly shook her head. "Tiny, since this is your special day, I'll just pretend I didn't hear that."

With a deep sigh and slowly shaking her head, Roberta turned back to recapture the setting sun. After another long, quiet moment, she gently tapped Tiny on his shoulder. When she spoke, her voice was as soft as the floating clouds above. "My, oh, my. What a colorful sky we have tonight. Simply marvelous. Tiny, on some rare occasions, you can see a fleeting, green light streak across the horizon. Maybe you and I shall be so fortunate. Wouldn't that be something with your very first sunset?"

Tiny had listened to every word, no longer feeling alone. He liked hearing a softer voice.

Together, side by side, they gazed at the beautiful evening sky in all its splendor. As the sun vanished from the jungle's sky, Rapid Roberta and Tiny Turtle hopped and crept off together, which is not easy for a bouncing Bunny and trudging Turtle to do. But because they wanted to, they could and did.

And for the moment all was well. Tiny, with his new teacher, forgot all about Roberta's unkind teasing. Gone, too, were Roberta's hostile thoughts of the Saber-toothed Tiger. But lessons unlearned have a way of coming back, causing painful consequences. And all too often life ending tragedies.

And in the jungle, lurking behind every shadow, there might be a threat, real or imagined, far greater than the streamlined Cheetah.

Chapter 5

Still strolling side by side they were on their way to Roberta's favorite meadow. And now with the hazy sun below the rim, darkness would soon rule the night. When she paused to enjoy the first, faint glow of a distant star, Tiny was moved to say something. "I'm hungry."

"I had my sunset," Roberta replied kindly, "and you shall have your dinner. Shall we dine?"

"You mean, you and - - -"

"Yep!" she interjected. "We'll have dinner together."

"I was going to say that. You sure talk fast," said Tiny as quickly as he could, afraid he might be interrupted again.

"I was just thinking how slow you talk. I guess if I'm going to be your teacher, we'll need to make a few *quick* adjustments."

Roberta was already thinking how she could change Tiny to better suit her style, when a determined voice broke in on her thoughts. "I'm hungry. When do we eat?"

"Er, soon Tiny. I was just - - -"

"But I'm hungry now and - - -"

"Soon!" she said firmly, turning to face him. "Just don't interrupt me."

Tiny's expression changed to a pout. "Are you angry with me?" he asked guardedly.

Almost before Tiny could complete his question, Roberta responded in her usual hurried manner, but in a tone more pleasant. "No. Not really. I guess I'm hungry, too. Usually, right before dinnertime I get a little cantankerous. That's when my sisters call me grouchy."

Again, Tiny tried to contain himself, but failed miserably.

"I don't mind being laughed at, little one. But I really don't like to be interrupted. Sometimes it makes me angry."

"I'm sorry," said Tiny, who for some strange reason was having an easy time keeping up with the hopping Roberta. That he liked.

"Tiny, I do accept your apology." Then quickly changing the subject, she said, "Now, look above you. For our first dinner together, we have a brightly lit sky."

Tiny glanced upward. "Oh, my. I've never seen so many stars."

"That may be true," replied Roberta, who, without realizing it, was hopping at a much slower pace than her usual style. "And not only do we have a starlit sky, we also have a full moon."

"My, oh, my," expressed a wide-eyed Tiny. "I do believe it's my very first."

"Well, my little pupil, if you stay with me, I guarantee that you'll have a variety of new experiences."

"I don't know if I'm ready for any more experiences," said a cautious Tiny.

"Well, you let me know when you're ready," she said pleasantly. "As your teacher, I would enjoy showing you my world. Now, for your special day, let's see if we can find some fresh, green leaves and a bunch of tender, red roots for dinner."

Although Roberta was talking as fast as ever, Tiny heard that clear and sure. "All right!" he cheered. "I'm ready to eat!"

Finding food in the jungle, where plants and fruit trees grew abundantly, was an easy and delightful chore. Their challenge was not to be someone else's meal while they were trying to enjoy theirs.

During their shared dinner, Tiny was toying with some thoughts of his own. "I know you said you could run faster than the Zebras. But can you run with the Cheetah?" As he waited for Roberta to reply, he swallowed a soft, green leaf.

Roberta's ears twitched anxiously. Deep in thought, her movements became deliberate. She put down her unfinished carrot and said somberly, "That streamlined Beast is built for lightning speed, faster than the wind itself. No Creature alive can outrun that feline freak. Those who try - - -" Her voice died off, not wanting to even think about being just one more helpless victim.

In spite of lingering thoughts of the Cheetah, both Roberta and Tiny enjoyed their dinner together. Even though they had a few obvious differences, there seemed to be a better understanding between them. Especially when it came to a handful of wild blueberries, which they shared for dessert.

"That was fun!" grinned Tiny, licking his blue lips. "Blueberries are my most favored food. I can't remember a yummier meal."

"My Mom says that meals always taste better when you eat out." As Roberta reminisced, a rare smile broke free. "And she's right, for there's nothing that can compare with the sweetness of the fruit picked right off the vine."

Tiny nodded as he put away a sweet, juicy blueberry.

"As for the blueberries, continued Roberta, "they're a sweet treat, but I can take 'em or leave 'em."

"Not me!" chimed in Tiny, almost biting his tongue while eating another one. "Blueberries *will* always be my favorite dessert."

Roberta and Tiny continued to do what they liked to do best. She talked on and on about her family, the sunsets, the trees, and of course, her favorite subject, herself. While Tiny, content just to listen, enjoyed helping a few more blueberries disappear.

Before they knew it, the full moon was high overhead, and one of them began to show a worried look. "It's getting late. I - - - I wanna go home."

"Relaxed, little one," Roberta said with that air of self-confidence. "You seem to enjoy worrying about nothing." She paused just long enough to glance at the sky. When she turned back to Tiny, she said pleasantly, "Tonight for your special day, we'll sleep under the stars. Doesn't that sound marvelous?"

"No," squeaked Tiny. "I wanna go home - - - now."

"Tiny, you'll be safe with me. And there's no way you could get home before sunup. No disrespect intended, but the way you creep along, you'll be up all night. Besides, there are night prowlers prowling about searching for a fresh, meaty meal. Sooo, relax and enjoy a night out with me."

"But I'm afraid."

"Tiny, remember what I told you. Fear is only a figment of *your* imagination. And in my favorite meadow, we'll be safe. Trust me."

Tiny, not knowing what to say remained silent, but his tummy was churning over and over. When feeling overwhelmed, he would always slip into his shell. It was instinctive. But for the moment, and not knowing why, he was able to resist that deeply ingrained impulse to hide.

Roberta turned from the glitter above and said softly, "Tiny, we have a beautiful night with a full moon and a sky twinkling with a thousand stars."

Quicker than a Beetle's wink, Tiny exclaimed, "How many stars?!"

Roberta gave Tiny a double look, then smiled to herself. "Oh, about a thousand or two, I'd say. Or, maybe a million," she added nonchalantly.

"Wow! A *million* stars!" blurted Tiny. But then with those persistent doubts, he said passively, "But I should go home."

Roberta could clearly see that Tiny's resistance was wavering. She moved in closer. "Here's your opportunity to enjoy a new experience, sleeping under a billion stars."

"Oh, my," uttered Tiny, his voice just above a whisper. "A *billion* stars." Then as he followed Roberta's lead, he gazed across the evening sky, there to see bright, flickering stars everywhere. He was completely enchanted.

"Then it's settled," Roberta affirmed softly. "You and I will spend our first night together under a billion stars."

Tiny nodded, as he gazed at all the sparkling lights above.

As time slipped by, Roberta continued to describe the wonders of the night. "Tiny, just try to imagine a zillion stars above each one glowing beyond compare."

Tiny, his eyes doing a little dance, was captivated by Roberta's description of the evening sky, home of a zillion stars.

Sometime later, Roberta was still sharing her adventures, while a tired Tiny was now beyond listening. Instead, he was involved with his own thoughts. "I wonder if her baby brothers and sisters ever call her Rapid-Mouth Roberta?" Approaching slumber, a pleasant smile captured Tiny's sleepy face.

The jungle's brilliant sky covered Roberta and Tiny like a warm blanket. While they slept, the night became alive. The sounds of Nature were everywhere. The wind sang its lullaby with the tall trees, and the shiny stars blinked their oft-told story to a vibrant Earth below. And as though on cue, the Creatures of the night, large and small, sang their favorite songs.

Every living thing is a part of the endless rhythm of Nature. And every sound is a voice that travels on the wind for all time. Those who care to listen, hear the secrets of the Universe.

Chapter 6

A restless Creature was stirring in the darkness of night. Straining to see through the eerie shadows, a feeble voice was heard. "R- - -Roberta. Are you awake?"

Roberta flicked her long ears. "I am now." Then, after a short pause, she added, "Are you okay?"

With a quiet sigh of relief, Tiny replied nervously, "I can't sleep. All those scary noises keep waking me up."

"What you are hearing are the beautiful sounds of Nature. We're being serenaded."

"Beautiful!?" blurted Tiny. "They're ugly!"

Roberta shrugged her shoulders, but couldn't keep back a faint smile. "What are ugly noises to you, is music to my ears."

"Well, for me, those noises are scary."

"Tiny," she said good-naturedly, "those sounds won't and can't hurt you. And I'm right here with you." Then with a playful tone in her voice, she added, "If those noises come after you, I'll protect you. I promise."

Teasing or not, Tiny was feeling better. "Thank you for not getting angry with me. I was almost afraid to wake you up."

Roberta's ears flicked. Before responding, there was a deliberate pause. Then, with a voice both serious and pleasant, she said, "Tiny, I don't want you to be afraid of me. Friends are to help each other. In a true friendship, there's no place for fear."

"*Friends* did she say?" grinned Tiny. "That's all I ever wanted. To have a friend. And someone to play with."

Their silence was brought to a close when Tiny heard his new friend saying, "I've learned something today, Tiny."

"Oh? What is it?"

"I learned that if fear is a waste of time, then so is getting angry. Who needs it?"

"I don't," agreed Tiny wholeheartedly.

"So, from this day forward, anger is a thing of the past. It's history. Starting now, I'm going to try to control my temper."

Tiny was elated. "I think that's a great idea. And a good lesson to learn, too." Then with his childlike voice, he ventured to ask, "Roberta, who's your teacher?"

Without a moment lost, Roberta replied proudly, "I am my own teacher." Then, after a long pause, she went on to say, "Actually, my parents and Mother Nature are my teachers. I observe and listen to everything around me. The trees. The sun and the wind. The rain and the grass. Everything. Sometimes I get so deep with my thoughts, I forget we live in a barbaric Jungle. Today it was an old Tiger that brought me back to my senses."

Tiny, not wanting to interrupt, waited before he asked his next question. "How did you get so smart so fast?"

"My Mom says I was born smart. That I'm precocious. Then, there are times she'll say I'm - - - obnoxious."

Tiny giggled. "Your Mom is pretty smart, too."

"Of that, I have no doubt, whatsoever," she replied sincerely. "My Mom is my constant inspiration. And Tiny, if you want to be my pupil, you need to know that all learning begins with being aware."

"Aware? Aware of what?"

"Everything. Awareness is the key to all learning. Without it, we remain as ignorant as a rock."

"Oh! I'll try real hard to remember that."

Following a reflective moment, Roberta said softly, "Tiny, I have a secret I would like to share with you."

Tiny perked up, surprised and delighted at the same time. "I like hearing secrets."

"Deep down inside," Roberta began, sounding very mysterious, "I have a soft, knowing voice that helps me to understand. It was my inner voice that said words couldn't hurt me."

Roberta looked upward to gaze at the bright stars, then back to Tiny. "It was also my inner voice that told me to go back to see if you were still in that hole. My Mom calls her inner voice, female intuition. That's my secret and you may share it with all of your friends, if you like."

Tiny slowly nodded his head, even though he knew he didn't completely understand what Roberta meant by female into-whatever she called it. But he was more than pleased knowing that Roberta shared her secret with him. At that moment, he was feeling very special. First a new name. Now a new friend. Once again, Tiny could feel the chills go up his back.

There followed a long pause. For the moment, the only sounds to be heard were those of the night.

"Roberta, I need help."

"Sure, Tiny. That's what teachers do."

"Well, I think I heard my parents say that the big will destroy the weak, and -"

"Whoa!" jumped in Roberta. "I'll be happy to help. But first I need to correct you."

"Oh, I thought I was on to something."

"Almost, Tiny. It's the strong Meat Eaters who are out to devour the weak."

"That's what I said," Tiny replied, sounding a bit confused.

"*Strong*, not big," assisted Roberta. "Some of my friends are big. There's Edi and Eddy Elephant. And there's Glenn Giraffe, who is so kindhearted, he won't even step on an Ant or swat a Fly."

"Thank you, Roberta. I'm beginning to understand."

"Tiny, you are a good pupil. I do enjoy being your teacher - - - immensely."

Tiny beamed. "I like compliments."

"And Tiny, remember that in this insensitive kingdom, crying is seen as being weak. So be careful."

Tiny slowly nodded his head. "I like Roberta's law that says crying is okay."

Roberta couldn't resist a rare smile, but in the dark of night, it remained hidden.

"Roberta, what about the law that says no blood, no pain?"

"Oh, you heard that? Well, I just made that up at the spur of the moment."

"I really don't like the sound of that one," Tiny said cautiously, afraid he might upset his new friend.

"To tell you the truth, I don't either. At least, not any more."

Tiny liked hearing that and he let loose a big smile.

Momentarily, a peaceful stillness encircled the two companions.

"Roberta?"

"Yes, Tiny."

"Thank you for taking the time to show me a part of your world. You're a good teacher."

Roberta's long ears went limp. She then took a deep breath to regain her composure. It didn't take her long. It never did. But by the time she responded with her own gratitude, Tiny was fast asleep under his zillion, shining stars.

Chapter 7

With eyes still closed, her ears began to flick. Birds of different colors were singing their early morning wake up call. Roberta arose from her slumber to see a Bluebird dancing on the wind. To her left she saw a Hummingbird sipping nectar from a honey-gold flower. "Ah, to be a part of Nature," she thought aloud. " What a marvelous way to begin a new day."

Then without another word, Roberta jumped up and turned to the East, preparing for a special moment. Prior to now, no matter how hard she had tried, she had always failed to wake up before the sun. With increasing anticipation, she thought aloud. "In a few moments, I'm going to capture my morning star, my very first sunrise. This will make my whole day."

Tiny opened his sleepy eyes, which were no larger than tiny green peas. With his first glimpse of a gray morning, he was not impressed. "I'm hungry," he yawned. "Let's have breakfast!"

There was no immediate reply. Tiny was about to call out again, when Roberta turned to face him. "In a few moments there will be a sunrise, my very first. There's plenty of time for breakfast. Why, you and I can enjoy this experience together and have a marvelous treat for the eyes."

Tiny missed hearing Roberta's excitement and said, "The only treat I need are some sweet blueberries."

"Well, it's time you raised your level of interest above your stomach. Is food your only interest?"

"I only think of food when it's time to eat. And right now my tummy tells me that I'm hungry."

Roberta, who had turned back to the empty horizon, again faced Tiny. She could feel a tug of frustration. "How can you think of food when there's going to be a beautiful sunrise?"

"Sunrise?" Tiny replied with indifference. Then, with increasing determination: "I'm hungry. And I want to eat now!"

Roberta slowly shook her head, resigned that her special moment was lost forever. "I guess there's no way I can enjoy my morning star with one hungry nuisance around."

Tiny's little eyes blinked, now realizing that Roberta was one grouchy Rabbit. "I'm sorry, but does that mean we can eat now?" he said hopefully, tilting his head to one side.

Roberta flicked her long ears. "Yeah, let's do it." She glanced over her shoulder to see that her morning star was beyond the horizon. Her disappointment was now complete.

There was a rustle of leaves. Tiny was already searching for some tasty morsels for breakfast. Roberta could only let out a deflated sigh, while Tiny had the look of contentment.

Chapter 8

"Win some, lose some," sighed Roberta. With a deep breath, she took a few moments to regain her composure. It didn't take her long. It never did. She knew enough not to let her disappointment ruin her whole day. "There will be other days to capture my morning star," she thought to herself. "Now it's time for breakfast. It will give me a chance to work on Tiny. He needs more help than I realized. But I know I'm up to it. I'm sooome Rabbit!"

In her paw, she held a ripe, red beet, but her thoughts were elsewhere. "How did you sleep last night, Tiny?" Not waiting for a reply, she continued. "Didn't you enjoy sleeping under the stars? It was so mar - - - ve l- - - lous."

Tiny looked pleased as he took his time to lick the early morning dew from a tender leaf. "Wel-l-l, not really," he replied slow and easy. "Hmmm, that was good," he smacked, as a fresh leaf disappeared, only to be replaced by another one. Savoring each bite, he stated, "I liked the part about the *zillion* stars. And that you were there to help me with my learning. But I missed being home with my parents. And those noises kept waking me up all night long."

Again Roberta flicked her long ears, feeling a bit impatient. "He sure does talk slow," she said to herself. "I'll have to do something about that and *quick*. If he is to remain my pupil, he'll need to accept my style."

Roberta took a moment to observe her little pupil, amazed at all the food he could eat. Now it was a tasty root big enough, she imagined, to stuff a giant Gorilla.

Caught up in her thoughts, Roberta absentmindedly picked up a red leaf and said, "Tiny, those noises we heard last night are the beautiful sounds of Nature. And if you listen with an open mind, you can learn to enjoy the sounds as I have."

Tiny nodded as though he was listening, but he went right on munching, content not to say a word.

"Tiny, you don't seem to understand, but those jungle noises are the songs of life. Each sound has its own special rhythm. My Mom believes that the sounds of the jungle are the heartbeat of life."

While Roberta tried to convince Tiny that their world was more than just a huge fruit salad, he didn't seem to be at all impressed. He just went right on finding more tasty tidbits to eat.

Following a long delay, Roberta turned to look directly at Tiny, who was now enjoying his favorite dessert. Turning down his offer of wild blueberries, thoughts continued to rush through her mind: "He doesn't seem to have any appreciation for Nature except eating. There's a whole world to enjoy, and all he can do is think of food. And because of him, I missed my first sunrise."

Unable to sit still any longer, Roberta jumped up and started hopping about. And while Roberta was spending her energy on Tiny's behavior, Tiny was content with his own happy thoughts. Now he was savoring a few more blueberries with a very loud SMACK.

"Now, there's a noise I can do without," she stated loud and clear. But Tiny went right on enjoying himself as though he hadn't heard a word.

Thinking to herself, Roberta slowly shook her head. "Changing him may be a waste of my time. But I'm not ready to give up on my little pupil. Not yet. He really does need me. I'll just have to change my approach - - - maybe."

Letting go a heavy sigh, Roberta flopped to the green clover. After some deep thought, she decided to use a different ploy. "Tiny," she began with renewed determination, "just take a deep breath and enjoy the sweet fragrance that is all around us."

"My joy comes from tasting, not smelling, " Tiny replied with a big yawn.

"Tiny," she continued, now with a touch of urgency in her voice, "don't you realize that we are surrounded by the wonders of Nature? Just open your eyes and take a good look."

Tiny took his good time to look about. "Now that my tummy is full, I do seem to see better. And the flowers do have pretty colors. But if you can't eat them, what good are they?"

A frustrated Roberta flicked her long ears. She decided to change the subject, which she was discovering was a lot easier than changing Tiny. Some other time she would try again to convince him that she was right. For some reason this was something she just had to do. Besides, she could help him realize all the beauty he was missing.

Roberta's thoughts were interrupted when she heard Tiny say, "I want to thank you for not getting angry with me. But when my tummy tells me it's time to eat, that's what I want to do."

Tiny, I understand." After a moment of hesitation, Roberta scratched her fury head and added, "I think."

"Well, that's a start," grinned Tiny.

Roberta gave Tiny a puzzled look, then cracked a smile. "Tiny, I think you like playing with my mind."

"Who me?" countered Tiny with a look of innocence.

"Yes, you my little pupil."

Tiny blushed, then said sincerely, "I'm sorry you missed your sunrise. Your morning yellow."

"Morning star," she corrected, slowly shaking her head.

"Well, I am sorry."

"I know you are, and I do accept your apology. And it's okay, Tiny. There's always tomorrow. I'll just keep on trying."

Tiny lowered his green eyes and said softly, "Roberta, I like you. Thank you for being my friend."

There followed a long, uneasy silence. Roberta shifted her attention to a pair of fluttering Butterflies. When she turned back, Tiny held out his little hand.

"Er, thank you Tiny." And together they shared a few, sweet blueberries.

Their breakfast completed, they picked themselves up from the meadow's yellow-green carpet. Strolling together, Roberta was enjoying the role of the teacher, while Tiny was content just to ask questions and listen.

But this is the Jungle Kingdom where at any moment lurks the threat of danger. And for those who forget, even for an instant, painful lessons are to be learned. Suddenly, and without warning, a fierce, yellow blur streaked through the air aimed at Roberta.

"Look out!" screamed Tiny, as he shot deep into his shell.

Roberta, her reflexes sharp and true, jumped to one side to escape the clutches of the charging Beast. It was the Cheetah.

The separation between life and death had never been closer. Too close for Roberta, and her ears thumped wildly. When she heard the Cheetah's roar, her fear intensified.

Tiny, trembling in his shell, was terrified as never before.

Roberta focussed her full attention on the wild demon. Her instinctive impulse was for survival. But there was also an inner force not to leave Tiny.

Missing his prey was no real concern for the proud and confident Cheetah. Separated by only a long reach, the spotted feline flashed a toothy smile at his helpless victim. Their eyes locked. For the hungry Beast, the fun was just beginning. "So, they call you Rapid Roberta, do they? Well, for me, you're just a mere tidbit to entice my appetite."

Even though escape seemed hopeless, Roberta was prepared to dash off. But no one outruns the fastest Creature alive. Then, no longer than it would take to blink, Roberta diverted her attention to Tiny. At that very moment, the Cheetah slashed out with his sharp, pointed claws to snatch his helpless prey.

But Roberta was gone. Instinctively, with the Cheetah's first move to strike, Roberta had darted off with one of her jack-rabbit starts. The chase was on.

With an ominous roar, the big Cat took off after his prey. The arrogant Cheetah sneered, "Your fate is now in my claws. My fangs like scorpions will sting your furry hide. And what I threaten, I do." His scowl was swept away with a confident grin. "Now we shall see how fast you are, bouncing Bunny."

A terrified Roberta, now had only one thought: SURVIVAL!

The Cheetah began the fatal chase with an easy, natural gait. Then, without any apparent effort, the wild Beast put on his blistering speed, sensing a quick victory. This time there would be no escape.

For Roberta, it was the chase she never wanted. Her desire to live was never stronger. But there was no way she could outrun the streamlined Cheetah.

The spotted Cat reached lightning speed. With each powerful stride, he drew closer to the zigzagging Roberta. Now, only a heated breath away, the Cheetah gauged where Roberta would be and projected his leap perfectly. His graceful flight through the air was straight and true. On impact, a violent rumble could be heard, and a cloud of blinding dust rose high above the ground.

When the dust settled, Roberta was nowhere to be seen. The roar of the Beast thundered through the jungle.

A terrified Tiny peered out from his shell to see if Roberta had escaped the enraged Cheetah. But there was no Roberta. Tears filled his eyes. "Poor Roberta. What a terrible, terrible nightmare. Poor Roberta."

There was a snap of a branch. Tiny raised his head just high enough to see. And there, not too far away, stalked the spotted Beast. Tiny stared motionless, afraid to even breathe.

The Cheetah stopped only a few feet away. With the fear of making a sound, Tiny dared not slip back into hie shell. The jungle Cat looked about. Then, unaware of Tiny's presence, he moved deeper into the brush.

An eerie stillness consumed the grassy meadow. Now that the Cheetah was no longer in sight, Tiny again peered over the grassland, not wanting to accept what he feared to be true . But there was no Roberta. The stillness was lost with broken sobs. "Roberta. My Roberta gone forever."

Chapter 9

A deafening screech split the air. The Cheetah, with wounded vanity, decided to call it a day. With vengeance on his mind, the spotted Beast snarled with contempt. "Bouncing Bunny, you and I will meet again. Your days are numbered. And I *will* strip you of your furry hide." With an arrogant glare, the sleek feline vanished into the jungle as quickly as he had appeared.

Some distance away, a Creature peered cautiously from the tall shrubs that surrounded the meadow. Without making a sound, she searched her surroundings. It was Roberta.

Exhausted, Roberta took a deep breath. Still looking about, she knew that the Cheetah would need no excuse to charge back for vengeance. This was no time for a victory cry. But it was a good time to give thanks to the Great Spirit. And she did.

She let go a heavy sigh. "No reason to aggravate an already ill-tempered Beast," thought Roberta. "I heard your threats and I *will* remember. I am a SURVIVOR!"

Quicker than a Hornet's sting, Roberta gasped. "Oh, my thumping ears! Where's Tiny?!"

Calling out his name, Roberta anxiously started her search. Stretching out her neck to the limit, she looked in every direction. But there was no Tiny. Frantically, she retraced her steps, unsure of what she might find, but hoping that Tiny was safe and unharmed.

Darting quickly through the brush, and still calling out his name, she stopped short, her ears twitching. She turned in the direction sensed by her keen hearing. She stared hard and something in the distance caught her eye. Without a moment wasted, Roberta took off, calling, "Tiny! Tiny! Are you all right?!"

Still sobbing, Tiny glanced up, not believing his eyes. Overjoyed, he cried out, "It can't be! But it is! "You're Roberta!"

"Hey, hey. Slow down Tiny. It's okay to cry, but only if there's a need. And as you can see, I'm still here." Then, with her furry paw, Roberta gently brushed away a flood of tears. "I'm just relieved that you're all right, too."

"But Roberta, how did you escape the Cheetah? I thought I would never see you again. I was scared to death!"

"Well, I wasn't scared. I stood right up to that over-spotted demon, showed him my terrific rabbit punch, and he ran off with his tail between his legs like a timid scaredy-cat." While describing her miraculous escape, Roberta had doubled up her paw into a fist, waving it high over her head as though ready to clobber some imaginary foe.

It was an impressive story, but Tiny was not nearly convinced. "But, Roberta. Er, ah. Are you telling me that - - -"

"Hey, hold on," interrupted Roberta with a wide grin. "You're talking pretty fast for a tiny Turtle. Did the big, vicious Beast scare you so terribly that you forgot who you are?"

Tiny stood his ground. "Are you teasing me about being afraid?"

"Who me?" she responded guardedly, surprised by Tiny's assertive behavior. "Why, no. Of course not. Er, I just meant that you sounded afraid. That's all."

"Well, I was terrified. And I was terrified for you, too!"

"You were?" said Roberta, sounding somewhat subdued.

"I sure was," replied Tiny, his eyes getting bigger as he spoke. "When I saw that Cheetah take after you, I thought you were - - -" Tiny stopped. He didn't even want to give it a second thought. Then, his voice changed to one of gratitude. "I'm just happy you're alive."

Then surprising them both, Tiny spontaneously jumped up and gave Roberta a big hug. When he let go, Roberta stepped back, blushing profusely. She was completely caught off guard by Tiny's show of affection. And for her, she was feeling extremely discombobulated.

"Well, er, ah, Tiny - - -" Roberta wavered, trying hard to regain her composure. "I - - - I didn't know you were so concerned about my safety. But I'm a big girl and I can take care of myself. But I do appreciate your - - -"

Roberta faltered again. After a long, awkward moment, and still feeling uneasy, she wasn't sure of what to say. "Well, ah. How are you feeling, Tiny?"

"Oh, I'm fine now. The Cheetah never gave me a second look. It was your life that was in danger, not mine."

While Tiny was sharing his thoughts, Roberta was still preoccupied with restoring her composure. It was taking a little longer than usual.

"Roberta, are you all right? Are you listening?"

"Er, yeah. Of course I'm listening."

"Well?"

"Well, er, what?" she replied trying not to look flustered, but failing miserably.

Tiny tilted his head and looked at her suspiciously. "How did you really get away from that Cheetah?" Then, looking directly at Roberta, he said softly, "I want to know the truth. You can trust me."

Roberta, still struggling with mixed feelings, took a deep breath. Appearing to have regained her composure, she stood tall and said, "Well, what really saved me was my skill of zigging and zagging, and knowing how to change directions on a thin whisker. I do it instinctively. So, I'm here with you because of my famous jack-rabbit starts and not my rabbit punch. I'll save my punch for that low-down, ludicrous Lizard that lives in the swamp."

Tiny flinched, but ever so slightly that Roberta failed to notice it. Choosing to ignore her remark, Tiny went on to say, "I know you're much braver than I am."

Roberta was all set to agree. But unlike her style, she thought for a moment before responding. "Tiny, the Great Spirit gives to everyone a means of survival. So it's not a matter of who's braver. What really matters is that you and I are here to talk about it. We are survivors!"

"But weren't you scared at all?" asked Tiny. "While hiding in my shell, I heard your ears thumbing."

Roberta closed her eyes, slowly shaking her head. "Won't I ever learn to hide my feelings?" thought Roberta. When her ears began to twitch, she tried so hard to control them, that her face became distorted.

"Are you all right, Roberta? You don't look so good."

Tiny's concern was so real, that Roberta was beginning to feel uneasy all over again. "Er, yes. I'm okay. I was just thinking."

Tiny moved in a little closer. "Roberta, if it's okay to cry, then it's okay to be afraid."

"Is that Tiny's law?" she said, still trying to regain her composure.

"I don't know," he replied shyly. "Maybe."

Roberta let loose a heavy sigh. "To tell you the truth, my ears were thumping because I was terrified. No one outruns that Cat, not even Rapid Roberta. Zigging and zagging, and a lot of fast praying saved my hide from the claws of that arrogant Beast. For me, the chase was a terrifying nightmare that I never want to experience again. Never!"

"Thank you for trusting me," said Tiny, still looking up to Roberta.

"Sure, Tiny. That's what friends are for." Then with that glint in her eye, she boasted, "But I sure showed that feline freak a thing or two."

"Well, the Cheetah sure got a good look at your fluffy cottontail," laughed Tiny.

Surprised by Tiny's gumption, Roberta took a long look at her laughing companion. Then saying with an amused grin, "That was real cleaver of you. And Tiny, I do like your spunk."

Tiny beamed. "And I do like compliments!"

"And numbers," laughed Roberta.

Tiny smiled. "I like it when you put on a happy face."

Roberta shrugged. "I do tend to take life too seriously. But that seems to be my nature."

"Maybe," Tiny said with a shrug of his own. "And I thank you for being honest with me. I feel better knowing that I wasn't the only one afraid of the Cheetah. And to know that fear is more than just a feeling in my tummy."

"That's for sure. I guess my ears knew it before I did."

Tiny nodded his agreement. Then, cautiously he asked, "Roberta, do friends lie to their friends?"

Without any hesitation, Roberta responded. "Tiny, right off hand, I can't remember telling you a lie. But I do exaggerate from time to time."

"Why?"

"When I'm in charge of eleven baby Bunnies, on occasion I need to exaggerate to prove a point or to stay in control."

"You do it so well, Roberta."

"What's that? Exaggerate?" she asked with a sly grin.

"No. Staying in control," Tiny quickly replied.

Roberta's grin broke into a short laugh. Then, only half joking, "Tiny, you're growing so fast, that you're going to force me to a higher level. Or, maybe I'll just need to retire as your teacher."

"I know I'm learning a lot. And I'm glad you're my friend and teacher. You have shown me a whole new world."

"That's what teachers do. And to help each other when in need. Or in a *hole*," she added with a wink.

Tiny blushed, still not knowing how to respond to her teasing.

Then, as though she knew what to do, Roberta led Tiny to a shady spot in the meadow.

Sitting together, face to face, they were hidden from the warm, midday sun. There was an unusual moment of peaceful quiet. The only sounds were those of the wind, rustling its way through the nearby trees.

Moments passed by before her voice entered the silence. "Tiny, I learned three things today."

"Oh?" Tiny replied with surprise and curiosity. "What are they?"

"First, that fear is more than a figment of our imagination."

"I knew it!" Tiny perked up, his eyes doing a little dance.

"What I felt when chased by that streamlined Cat was real and terrifying. Yes, Tiny, you were right and I was - - - well, let's just move on."

After a long pause to collect her thoughts, she continued. "Second, that friends need to be honest with each other. And it feels so good."

Tiny agreed wholeheartedly and nodded with gusto.

"Third, the Great Spirit does provide: My gift of speed and your protective shield."

Before going on, Roberta reached over to touch Tiny's shoulder. Her words came slow, and at times uneven. "Tiny, I want to apologize for all those unkind remarks I said about you and your shell. I was completely out of line. I was speaking out of anger and having a little fun."

"Roberta, I forgave you when you were helping me find a new name."

Taking her time, Roberta gave Tiny a close look. "Thank you, Tiny. I'm beginning to see that I have a lot to learn about being a *true* friend."

Roberta, now feeling overexposed, took a deep breath and folded her arms across her lap. "As I was saying, the gifts provided by our Great Spirit made it possible for you and me to survive a life and death experience. For that, our relationship will never be the same."

Tiny slowly nodded his head. "I know that I feel different, but I don't have the words to express it."

Following another quiet moment, Roberta inquired, "Why the big smile, Tiny?"

"Oh, I'm just happy that I'm learning to trust you more and more. It feels so warm."

Freeing up her arms, Roberta said softly, "Trust is very important if a friendship is to grow."

Tiny, now smiling with pride, shared his deepest thought: "It also feels good to know that my friend is by far the zigzaggiest Rabbit in the whooole kingdom."

"Well, I knew that," said Roberta, flicking her fluffy cottontail. "Now you and that pompous brute know it, too. But no matter, I just didn't relish the idea of being the Cheetah's lunch."

"Or me being his mock turtle soup," Tiny said with laughter.

Roberta smiled. "I really do like your spunk."

Tiny beamed. "And I really do like compliments."

"Stay with me, Tiny, and you'll go far."

At that moment, neither one knew exactly how true her casual remark would prove to be. But perhaps, not the way Roberta had intended.

Once again, lost in her thoughts, Roberta truly believed that she was a good influence for Tiny. She was delighted to be his teacher and friend. And the belief of her own importance was never stronger then at that very moment.

Without a doubt, it had been quite an eventful morning for Roberta and Tiny. And from her way of thinking, she had plenty of reason to be grateful. In her eyes she was sooome Rabbit!

Chapter 10

Roberta's contentment was short-lived when Tiny said, "I wonder when the Cheetah will attack again?"

Quicker than a Cobra's strike, Roberta leaped high off the ground. Her long ears were pointed upward like two straight arrows without a quiver. "Jungle!" she vented, her ears now thumping with passion.

Tiny had already disappeared into his shell, afraid that the vengeful Cheetah had returned.

This time there was no danger. It was only a very angry Roberta. There was fire in her voice. "We live in a Jungle where no Rabbit, Turtle, or Mouse is safe! We're in constant danger of being attacked. As long as we live under brute force, no one will ever be safe from a violent death! No one! We almost got killed today! Can't anyone hop through the meadow without being ambushed by some mean, vicious Beast?!"

Tiny was overwhelmed. Never had he heard such anger in Roberta's voice. So much so, he decided to stay right where he felt secure - - - deep inside his shell.

Gripped by her own anger, Roberta hadn't noticed that Tiny had retreated into his shell. And with heated passion, she continued her tirade. "We live in a Jungle where every Creature has become so self-centered that no one is aware of the needs of others. Because of hate and greed, the Meat Eaters have taken over! Today, it's kill or be killed! We live and die in a world where the ruthless destroy the weak!"

"T- - -That's me," stuttered Tiny, slipping deeper into his shell. But he couldn't escape hearing Roberta's agitation.

"It's time something was done to put an end to all this violence," she shouted. "Who needs it?!"

"I don't," squeaked Tiny.

"Of course not!" she cried out, still unaware of Tiny's plight. "No one needs it! We are destroying ourselves, but no one seems to care anymore! It's everyone out for themselves!"

"But I'm too afraid to come out," uttered Tiny.

"Yes! There are many who are too afraid to come out for change! For thousands of years we have lived with this senseless fear. But as long as we live under the law of tooth and claw, we are all doomed! This madness has to be stopped!"

Roberta stopped. She was out of breath, overcome by her own heated zeal.

Tiny, still deep inside his shell, cocked his head and listened. But all he heard was the pounding of his own heart. He slowly peaked out of his shell, his eyes blinking from the sun. "A *thousand* years did you say? Wow! That's a long, long time." Then, feeling exposed to the dangers of the jungle, he darted back into his shell.

With renewed passion, and still with her head held high, Roberta continued. "Violence has been a way of life for countless generations. But now it's time for change. Why can't we all learn to live together, to be friends rather than enemies? Someone should do something before it's too late. Our *jungle* has become a heartless *Jungle*!"

Quicker than a thunderbolt lights the sky, Roberta was struck with an idea. "That's it!" she declared, her voice filled with conviction. "You and I will lead the way. Our friendship will be an example for others. Together we will show our kingdom how to live in peace and harmony."

Tiny inched out of his shell and said weakly, "We?"

"Yes, we!" repeated Roberta, too excited to hear the fear in Tiny's voice. "We're going to help create a world where everyone is safe from violence."

Cautious by nature, Tiny was certain about one thing: He wanted no part of Roberta's scheme, whatever it was.

"Just think of it, Tiny. I have created a worthy cause that we can't allow to fail. We can call it the Great Crusade. A Crusade to save our Jungle Kingdom from self-destruction."

A worried expression captured Tiny's face. "I don't think I'm ready for a great crusade. Home and a good meal sound safer."

Roberta put her paw around Tiny's shoulder. "Tiny, do you remember our pledge for courage and wisdom? Well, here's our opportunity to grow and to do something worthwhile for our kingdom. Think of the fame and glory."

Tiny wanted to do the right thing, but his nagging thoughts just wouldn't go away. "Glory I don't need. But I would like to grow. And doing something for our kingdom does sound nice. But what can we do?"

"It will be a difficult task," began Roberta, the excitement still in her voice. "First, we will need to make a request for the Grand Assembly. There all the adult Animals will have the opportunity to vote to change our violent kingdom to a peaceful paradise."

"Will it be dangerous?" mumbled Tiny, trying hard to push aside his fearful thoughts.

"It might be," replied Roberta with that air of confidence. "But greater the risk, greater are the rewards for growth and glory. Besides, we'll have the blessings of our Great Spirit." She paused for a moment, then said softly, "Tiny, I'll be at your side and I promise to take good care of you no matter what dangers we might face. Trust me."

"I do trust you. If not, I would have been home long ago. I'm just a slow learner, and it takes me longer to think things through."

"Tiny, I'm amazed at your growth," she said sounding sincere. "You're no longer the timid Tiny I first met. Today you have spunk. And now you and I have an opportunity to grow to a higher level. I guess what it comes down to is this: do we have the courage to take on this monumental challenge?"

An uneasy silence filled the air. It was obvious that Tiny was trying hard to make up his mind. At the moment, Roberta didn't know what more to say. So, she decided to wait quietly, which for her was a real challenge.

Tiny, taking his time, eventually turned to Roberta. "I guess if I want to keep on growing, I'll need to stick my neck out." Then, and still with a degree of uncertainty, he said gingerly, "Okay. I'll do it."

Roberta was on the verge of giving Tiny a big hug, but it remained only a passing thought. After thanking him, she gave Tiny an affectionate touch on his shoulder. "Tiny, I really do need your support. And working together, we could make a difference."

Tiny slowly nodded his head, but there was a look in his eyes that seemed to imply that he had something on his mind.

For Roberta, it was obvious that she was in deep thought. With growing excitement, she was already planning their next step for her Great Crusade. But the presumptuous Roberta was again moving too fast for Tiny, who had a question that would prove disturbing.

"Roberta, when you say that *all* the Animals will be invited to the Grand Assembly, does that mean the Cheetah, too?"

Roberta flicked her long ears. Leaning over, she peered down her pink nose. "Tiny, that's a foolish question. Please don't vex me."

Tiny held his ground. "You promised you would control your temper."

Roberta stood straight up. When she spoke, her voice was firm and steady. "Tiny, you know I keep my promises. If you remember, I said I would *try* to control my anger. And our Great Spirit knows I've been trying."

"I know it, too," said Tiny. "But what about the Cheetah?"

"Tiny, that spotted savage almost had me for lunch. Then, he threatened to have my furry hide if it was the last thing he did. I hope I never see that vengeful Beast again. There's no way that I'd be able to escape his sharp claws a second time. No way!"

Again Tiny nodded, but he was still determined to share his concern. "I just can't see how you plan to have a Grand Assembly for all the Animals, and at the same time, not to include the Cheetah."

"Tiny, I understand what you're saying. But I know what I'm doing. Trust me."

"Roberta, you are my best friend and I do trust you. I just think you're making a mistake."

Roberta took a close look at Tiny. Her ears began to twitch. But then with a half grin she said, "Tiny, let's agree to disagree and move on. And I do like your spunk."

This time, Tiny didn't respond with his usual reply. And with each word, his voice became stronger. "Well, you do have my support. And I promise I'll try to do my very best."

"I know you will, Tiny. Of that, I have no doubt. And I do appreciate your support. You and I are on our way. Working together, side by side, my Great Crusade can't fail."

"I hope you're right, Roberta."

"So do I, Tiny. So do I."

Privately, their thoughts were far apart. "If she excludes the Cheetah," thought Tiny, "her plan seems doomed to failure before it starts."

Roberta's thoughts were much more optimistic than Tiny's, but maybe not as realistic: "I won't let my mission fail without doing all I can to make it a success. And the Great Spirit willing, my Crusade will be triumphant!"

Chapter 11

"Now to put my plan into action," shared Roberta, her voice filled with *zealous* conviction. "We are going into the Dark Forest to find Cyrus the Great Horned Owl."

"We are?" asked Tiny, not at all sure that's what he wanted to do. Having a snack sounded better. And much safer.

"Yes we are," asserted Roberta. "We are going to request the Grand Assembly of *all* the Animals, with the obvious exclusion of one beastly Beast."

Roberta hesitated, but Tiny had already decided not to belabor the point about the Cheetah . He just couldn't understand how Roberta's crusade could succeed if she excluded the Cheetah. From his way of thinking, Roberta was heading for a big disappointment. But how do you tell a friend who would rather argue than listen?

When Roberta was satisfied that she would not be interrupted, she proceeded. "As I was saying, the Animals will be cordially invited to attend the Grand Assembly. There they will hear my plan to create a kingdom where everyone will be able to hop, strut, gallop, fly, or slither. Or," she added with a wink, "even creep without fear."

Tiny flinched, but he held back his hurt feelings. He still had a difficult time accepting Robert's teasing, even though he knew she meant no harm. "I wonder who is going to grow up first?" thought Tiny to himself.

Roberta glanced over to his little companion, and could see his preoccupation. "Tiny, if there 's going to be a long face in the crowd, let it be mine."

"Oh, I'll be all right. As I said before, I'm a slow learner."

"Well, for the moment, I have enough enthusiasm for us both. Just think of it, Tiny. You and I are on a Great Crusade to help turn our ruthless Jungle Kingdom into a paradise, a paradise without hate or violence. Doesn't my terrific plan sound terrific?"

"Yes, I guess so," he replied halfheartedly. There followed a deliberate pause, as though Tiny was deep in thought. "Roberta, may I make one suggestion?"

Roberta hesitated as she gave Tiny a long, curious look. Then sounding both surprised and delighted, she responded, "By all means. Please tell me."

Tiny took his time searching for the right words. "For our kingdom, could we also eliminate - - - starvation?"

Roberta's ears stood straight up. Then with that glint in her eye, she quickly replied, "With your appetite, I should have known. And Tiny, that's a very good suggestion. Let's do it!"

Tiny beamed. "I like compliments."

Roberta gave Tiny a favorable nod. "That's the Tiny I know." Then bringing her paw to her furry chin, she went on to say, "So, our request to the Grand Assembly will be to eliminate violence and starvation. So be it!"

"So be it!" repeated Tiny.

After a round of cheers, Tiny had a question for Roberta. "Whooo is the Owl?"

The usually serious Roberta, playfully hooted, "Whooo are you to ask?"

Tiny was elated and replied with his own spontaneous, squeaky hoot, "I'm the little Turtle whooo lives in the shell of darkness. That's whooo."

Their childlike laughter broke through the midday air. Tiny turned on a happy smile. For him, playing came naturally and he was eager for more.

But not so for Roberta. She was now feeling a bit foolish, and was ready to get back to the challenge of her Crusade. As quickly as she had let go, her playfulness was over. Turning to Tiny, her demeanor was once again serious. "That was fun, but I can't allow myself to get carried away. Remember, we're on a mission to save our kingdom. We must always keep that as our top priority."

Tiny shook his head vigorously, as he tried to voice his displeasure. But once again Roberta interrupted. "I'm sorry to disappoint you, but I really don't have the time to play. Time for play is time wasted. One should always be in control."

Seeing the hurt in Tiny's eyes, only reinforced her determination to make her point. But, then again those sad, little eyes. Roberta's tone became more pleasant, but she was still set on having her own way.

"Tiny, I think I know how you feel. But we can't allow foolishness to interfere with our quest. We must be willing to sacrifice our whims for our worthy cause. And we mustn't fail. To fail would mean more violence and more starvation. When our mission is completed, there will be plenty of time for you to play. Trust me."

"But who will I play with?" he pouted. "You're my only friend."

"Tiny, I truly believe there will be a day that you'll have friends galore."

"But how do you know that?"

"Just a deep feeling I have. My Mom calls it female intuition."

"Oh, that," he replied, still holding on to his doubts.

Eager to move forward with her Great Crusade, Roberta looked at Tiny, and said with a faint grin, "You get rid of your need to pout, and I'll try extra hard to control my temper. Agreed?"

Tiny thought for a moment, who was discovering that thinking for himself was getting easier, especially if he took his time. When he was ready with his answer, he raised his head up high and said, "Roberta, I accept your challenge. I do believe I win either way."

Again Roberta rubbed her furry chin, while giving Tiny a long look. "I do believe you're right. You're becoming quite observant. What happened to that shy, inhibited Tiny I use to know who would disappear into his shell if I yelled boo?"

"You told me that words don't hurt, and that if I wanted to survive in our kingdom, I would have to grow up. I owe it all to you."

Unlike her style, Roberta took her time to think that over. "Tiny, I'm usually quick to take the credit, but your growth is beyond me. And please don't ask me to explain it, because I can't. Maybe someday, but not now."

Then, quickly changing the subject, she stated, "But I can tell you about Cyrus the Great Horned Owl, who is considered the wisest of all the Animals, far none."

"What makes the Big Owl so smart?"

"Well, he has lived longer than most. And it is told that he sees and hears everything. And what he learns, he never forgets."

"How old is Cyrus the Horn?" asked Tiny with growing curiosity.

Roberta was amused, and at the moment, saw no need to correct Tiny, believing that he would eventually get Cyrus' name right. "Tiny, they say that Cyrus the Great is one hundred and twenty-six years old." (Roberta really didn't know his age.)

"Woo Hoo!" spouted Tiny, repeating the Owl's age. "He's older than my great-grandmother!"

"Tiny and his numbers," smiled Roberta to herself. "Now as I was saying," she continued, sounding very serious, "Cyrus the Great, because of his wisdom, has been given the sole authority to summons the Grand Assembly. There the Great Cyrus will present our proposal." (Once again, Roberta really doesn't know this.)

"Then what?"

"Then the Grand Assembly will vote for or against our plan. And for our proposal to be accepted, the vote must be unanimous."

"The Cheetah!" Tiny blurted.

"Now you know why we must exclude that sleek freak. And ready or not, it's time to begin our journey to find the Great Cyrus."

But Tiny wasn't quiet ready. With a tilt of his head, he stated gingerly, "Before we start our journey, may I make one more suggestion?"

Although again caught by surprise, Roberta was quick to reply, "Most certainly. I'm all ears."

"Can we have lunch first? I'm hungry."

Roberta twitched her pink nose. She was mildly disappointed that Tiny hadn't caught her joke about her ears. But knowing that they would be soon on their way, she replied good-naturedly, "My Pop said a journey should never start on an empty stomach. Or as in your case, on an empty tummy. Shall we dine?"

Since their narrow escape from the Cheetah, this was the most sensible thing Tiny could remember hearing from Roberta. Well, almost.

Then quick as a Robin's heartbeat, Tiny's face turned a pale green.

"Hey, Tiny! Why the frightful look? I'm all for having lunch. Are you okay?"

"I - - - I just remembered the ugly rumors about the Dark Forest," he shuddered. "You know. The curse."

"Oh, that," Roberta replied calmly. "Tiny, there are rumors that are true, and others that fall by their own weight. For me, the rumor that those who enter the Dark Forest go violently mad is completely unfounded. I'm not afraid of any curse. Cheetah, yes. Curses, no way."

"But how can you be so sure?"

"I just know," she asserted with her usual display of confidence. "Most curses are nothing more than a foolish superstition contrived by some Creature, long dead, who had nothing better to do. Just remember, there is no curse hovering over the Dark Forest. You and I won't go crazy mad."

"Are you absolutely sure there's no curse?" asked Tiny with a deep feeling of uncertainty.

"Yes, without a doubt. But it really doesn't matter, one way or the other."

"Why not?" Tiny asked, still worried and now deeply confused.

"Because you and I survived the Cheetah, we can survive the Dark Forest, curse or no curse. Besides, I'll be with you at all times, and I will protect you from all harm, real or imagined. Trust me."

Roberta reached over and softly touched Tiny with her furry paw. "Are you feeling better?"

"A little," he replied weakly.

"Good. Now clear out your head, and no more idle talk about curses. For what you think is what you get. So think positive like me and you'll have nothing to fear. And I promise to take good care of you. Okay?"

Tiny nodded, and felt better when Roberta gave him one more gentle touch.

Roberta smiled, thinking she had covered herself quite nicely, while Tiny still had a few nagging doubts that just - - - wouldn't - - - go - - - away.

"Now, are you ready for our lunch?"

To which, Tiny had no doubts. "Yes! I'm hungry!"

Roberta shook her head with laughter. "Now, why doesn't that surprise me?"

As they shared a couple of tasty red roots, they remained alert for danger. "Having lunch is fun, but only if you're not someone else's," said Tiny with his little eyes doing their dance.

Roberta nodded as she reached over to share a few tidbits. Tiny grinned, "Hmmm. Blueberries will always be my favorite snack."

A few more savory morsels and frequent glances over their shoulders made for a scrumptious but anxious meal. This was the reality of living with the threat of violence, the very thing Roberta hoped to change.

Suddenly, Roberta raised her head. Her long ears flicked.

Bewildered, Tiny watched her jump up and scamper off. Roberta came to a gradual stop. Her keen sense of hearing brought her directly to what she had heard. Delighted by her discovery, she took a long, refreshing drink from the cool, clear brook. "I must tell Tiny about this," she said to herself. And she did.

With Roberta looking on, Tiny dived into the brook. Under the water, his movements were quick and smooth. "What a unique way to get a drink," thought Roberta with a humorous smile. "His swimming is as natural as my famous jack-rabbit starts. Look at him go. The Great Spirit does truly provide. Now, with my furry body, I'll just take my drink the usual way."

Tiny, looking fresh and content, popped up to get a breath of fresh air.

"Hey, Tiny! You're a great swimmer! But we're wasting time! Let's get moving!"

Together, side by side, they left the meadow and disappeared into the Dark Forest. Unknown to Roberta and Tiny, they were taking their first steps into what would prove to be a daring adventure, an adventure that could bring them to a higher level of understanding or heartbreaking failure. Or in some strange way, maybe both.

Chapter 12

One by one the trees loomed up, then disappeared behind them. Tiny turned to look directly at the slow-hopping Roberta. He called to get her attention, but she continued glancing from right to left, then back again.

Tiny, puzzled by her bizarre behavior, was beginning to worry that something was terribly wrong. He called out again, but with the same results. He was then grabbed by a horrifying thought: Was Roberta going mad?

"Roberta!" Tiny called out, this time much louder. "Are you all right?"

Her ears flicked, but she continued turning her head from side to side. As they approached one of the medium-sized trees, she reached out with her soft, furry paws to feel the rough, knotted bark. "I hear you," she replied hauntingly. "And I never felt better."

Tiny gave a sigh of relief, but kept his little hands to himself, not wanting anything to do with those grotesque looking trees.

As they moved on, Roberta continued to touch each passing tree. From Tiny's point of view, her behavior was very peculiar. "I do believe she's gone over the edge," Tiny mumbled to himself. Deeply troubled, he called out, "Roberta, you're scaring me!"

On that very note, Roberta stopped. Turning to Tiny, she said, "I'm sorry. I was lost in deep thought, fascinated by these trees and their natural beauty."

"Oh, oh," said Tiny to himself. "She's going crazy. These trees are ugly. It's the curse."

Roberta turned to Tiny and smiled. "Tiny, remove that long look off your face. You're beginning to look like me. Let me be the serious one. Okay?"

Tiny slowly nodded his head, but he was still suspicious of her weird behavior. She just didn't seem to be the same Roberta.

"Now, if you're ready, Tiny, let's keep moving." And they did, side by side.

Sometime later, Tiny was again troubled by a few disturbing doubts. And even though he feared the worst, he just had to know the truth. "Roberta, are you losing your mind?"

Without missing a hop, Roberta took her paw from the bark of a tree, and gently reached around Tiny's shoulder. "Yes, Tiny. Without a doubt, my mind is going - - -going - - - gone."

"Oh, no!" squeaked Tiny. "What's going to happen to us?"

"Oh, no. Not that way. You misunderstood me. What I mean to say is that I'm fascinated by the natural splendor of these ancient trees. They're absolutely mar- - vel - - - lous."

Tiny disagreed completely, but he was somewhat relieved that his Roberta was still Roberta. He was also thinking that maybe these trees weren't as ugly as they looked.

After they had traveled a short distance, Tiny had a question. "How much further do we have to go?"

"I don't know - - - exactly. We just need to keep on movin' on."

"Where does the Owl So Great live?" Tiny asked with growing curiosity.

Her answer was prompt but vague. "To be completely honest, I don't know where Cyrus the Great lives - - - exactly."

Quicker than a Cheetah's sneer, Tiny's curiosity was consumed with doubts. "But then how do you hope to find the Big Owl?" he blurted.

"That's easy. We are to look for a sign which will let us know where to find the Great Cyrus."

"Oh," replied Tiny, but not completely satisfied with her answer. Then, following a long pause, he said, "What is the sign you're looking for?"

"Something truly special of that I have no doubt. But what it is I don't know - - - exactly."

At that point, Tiny was feeling a little confused. "Roberta, I know that I'm lost. But I do trust you. And because of you, I'm going to meet the Great Bird."

"Thank you, Tiny. As I said before, it's always best to be optimistic. Just remember, every step we take gets us closer to our destination."

"All right!" cheered Tiny. "Lead on!"

Roberta was overjoyed. To be a teacher was always considered far beyond her reach, or so she had been told by those far wiser than she. Even to dare dream such achievements for a girl living in the Jungle Kingdom was unthinkable. Especially when you are forced to live under the law of tooth and claw.

Then, too, there was her Great Crusade. For Roberta, everything was coming together perfectly. "Life can be beautiful!" she said to herself. "If my Mom and Pop, and all my loved ones could only see me now. I just know they would be so proud."

At that same moment, Tiny was thinking how lucky he was to have a teacher as smart as Roberta. "She really does want to be my friend," he said to himself. "And I'm learning so much about everything. Someday I might even learn to like a tree."

Roberta was feeling simply marvelous. Then, with her pink nose up in the air, she stumbled over a hard rock, losing her balance and composure. Quickly regaining both, she turned to see the slow but sure-footed Tiny and smiled. She couldn't help but admire his effort.

Shortly, one of them needed to stop. "Tiny, I need to gather my whereabouts."

Tiny looked up, and then all around. "It's getting darker."

"That's because the trees are getting bigger and taller. That's why we can't see my morning star."

"Oh, I hadn't noticed."

"Tiny," she began, her voice firm but caring, "do you remember the first step required for learning?"

Tiny rolled up his little eyes. It was obvious that he was trying hard to remember.

"Take your time," she offered patiently.

And he did. Moments later, with a sparkle in his eye, he said with certainty, "One needs to be aware."

Roberta nodded her head with pride and gave Tiny a pat on his shoulder. "That's right! Awareness is the first step to all learning."

"What's the second step?" asked an inquisitive Tiny.

"That's an intelligent question, my aspiring pupil. But at the moment, I don't know - - - exactly. I'm still working on that."

Tiny looked surprised but pleased. "No stories or exaggerations, Roberta?"

"Friends don't need to impress their friends, only strangers and their younger siblings." (Do you remember when the Rabbit had the habit of impressing others?)

"Is that a law of the Jungle or Roberta's?"

Roberta gave Tiny a double look. "You're getting mighty quick. And I do like your spunk."

Tiny beamed. "And I do like compliments."

Roberta gave a quick nod, then said with that serious tone, "Now I do need to look about to see where we are."

Tiny was just about to ask Roberta if they were lost, when his eyes enlarged to the size of green grapes. Then his body went limp. Right before his bulging eyes, Roberta had spun her furry head completely around from left to right.

Tiny was speechless and could only stare in disbelief. "H - - - How did she do that?" he mumbled to himself.

Before he could regain his senses, Roberta pointed with one of her long ears and declared, "That way is forward! Let's be movin' on!"

Still bedazzled, Tiny could only manage a feeble response. "It's getting darker with each step. How do you know where we're going?"

Roberta, marching on with her head held high, declared with her familiar cry, "Trust me!"

Tiny was in no condition to argue. Although he was fearful of what might be hidden in the gloomy darkness ahead, there was some consolation that at least one of them knew where they were going. Picking up his feet as fast as he could, he was soon at the side of the slow-hopping Roberta.

To see Tiny trying his very best, gave Roberta a wonderful feeling of appreciation for her little companion. And moving along at Tiny's speed was a minor inconvenience. For each step they took, brought them closer to Cyrus the Great. Or so she believed.

Although his mind was again playing with fearful thoughts, Tiny continued to rely on Roberta's leadership. Little did he know at that moment, Roberta was merely trusting her female intuition as she led the way into the dark unknown.

To reach their destination, Roberta would need to make all the right choices. Or like the other Creatures who had dared to enter the Dark Forest, Roberta and Tiny would also perish, never again to see home.

Chapter 13

Although anxious to find Cyrus the Great, Roberta remembered to keep her pace down for the slow but sure-footed Tiny. Actually, by accommodating Tiny's needs, it gave her more time to marvel over the natural beauty of the timeworn trees.

Tiny's perception, however, was far from reassuring. Surrounded by dark, gloomy shadows, eerie vision began to fill his head. Staring at these old, gnarled trees, they appeared to be sprouting a grotesque, twisted mouth and long, scrawny arms. At any moment, he feared he would be grabbed and devoured by one of these monstrous trees.

To rid his mind of these terrifying thoughts, Tiny turned to Roberta and said, "I'm hungry. When can we eat?"

"Tiny, do I have a surprise for you."

Tiny beamed. "I like surprises. What is it?"

"You'll see," she replied pleasantly.

"When?" he asked with growing excitement.

"Real soon. Trust me."

After going a very short distance, Tiny's anticipation was satisfied when Roberta found a suitable resting place. As Tiny let himself drop to the mossy ground, Roberta brought forth two red apples.

Tiny gave a big smile, and this time Roberta returned one of her own. "Thank you, Roberta. I do like surprises. Especially the kind you can eat."

When the apples had been consumed, Roberta presented Tiny with a large handful of his favorite dessert. "Blueberries!" cheered Tiny.

As Tiny enjoyed his dessert one by one, Roberta politely declined his offer. "Those I brought for you, Tiny."

"Thank you again," Roberta.

"All the thanks I need is to see you enjoying yourself." And that's exactly what Tiny did, savoring each delicious bite.

Sitting nearby, Roberta was trying to imagine a world free of violence. "And here I am," she thought to herself, "on my way with my good friend to do what we can do to make it come true. To be a teacher and a leader, what a marvelous life. I'm sooome Rabbit!"

But her self-gratification was short lived. No sooner had the last blueberry disappeared, when Tiny glanced up. "These old trees are the ugliest and scariest trees I've ever seen."

"Hey, Tiny, these trees are beautiful. Trees are a creation of Mother Nature. They're alive and growing just like you and me. Really, there's absolutely nothing to fear. Trust me." Then with a rare, playful laugh, she said, "These giant trees won't bite you. They're vegetarians!"

"Vega-what?" said Tiny.

Roberta stopped laughing, disappointed that Tiny had missed her joke - - - again. Slowly shaking her head, she sighed, "Skip it."

At that very moment, Tiny's face broke into a mischievous grin. "I can't skip, but I can creep."

Roberta flicked her long ears. But then her laughter soon joined with Tiny's. "That was real clever, Tiny. And I really do believe you enjoy playing with my mind."

Tiny, turning on that look of innocence, hooted, "Whooo me?"

Roberta, again caught off guard by Tiny's spunk, couldn't help but laugh. But this time alone.

A horrifying stare gripped Tiny's face. Alarmed, Roberta cried out, "Tiny! What is it?! Are you all right?!"

Tiny's hand shook, as he slowly pointed above Roberta's head. "That - - - that tree moved. I saw it move towards us. And that big ugly one over there, too."

"Oh," replied Roberta, trying her best to hide her amusement. "Tiny, your mind is playing tricks on you." She turned and casually glanced over at the trees, then back to Tiny. Even though it was difficult to take his vivid imagination seriously, the fear in his eyes gave her reason to pause. "Tiny, there's nothing to fear. They're trees, and trees don't have feet. Why, you know as well as I do, trees are rooted to one spot . They can't move even if they wanted to."

Even with the confidence in her voice, Tiny was not to be pacified this time, and his voice began to crack. "I saw those ugly things move towards us. These trees are monsters with long, tangling branches to reach out and rip us apart."

Roberta was beginning to have a few self-doubts about her ability to be a leader. She realized that it had been a long journey for Tiny, and maybe he had reached his breaking point. She had to do something - - - and quick. But what could she do?

"Tiny, I'm here with you. And I'll protect you from all harm, as I promised. But you must come to your senses and realize that trees can't hurt you. They're harmless. Why, just think of the stories these enchanted, old trees could tell us if they could only talk."

That thought, seeing a gigantic tree with a gaping mouth, only added to Tiny's turmoil. And his little body began to shake all over.

With her soft paw, Roberta reached over to comfort Tiny. But he couldn't stop trembling. Being in command, Roberta was learning, came with big responsibilities. Maybe too big for one young Rabbit.

Approaching panic, not a word was spoken. One wishing to go back home, the other wanting to move forward, and neither one knowing where they were - - - exactly.

Roberta was now feeling uneasy. Seeing Tiny afraid over the unthinkable notion that these trees were monsters out to tear them apart, gave her serious doubts of her own ability to cope with the situation. "Is Tiny losing his mind?" she thought with a touch of anxiety. "And if he is, what can I do? Maybe there is a curse."

Suddenly, Roberta spun around to stare at the surrounding trees. Standing in the gloomy shadows, and trying hard to keep her wits, she felt a cold, creepy feeling move down her spine. It then occurred to her that they were being leered at by a thousand demonic eyes. Was Roberta losing her mind? There was only one thing for her to do.

Like a flash, Roberta twirled and seized Tiny by his hand. "Hold on tight!" she screamed. "These monstrous trees are demons! We're getting out of here. NOW!"

With her jack-rabbit start, she turned on her speed, sprinting faster and faster, her ears thumping madly. There was no way that Tiny could run with Roberta. Still clutching her paw, he had lifted his legs off the ground and allowed himself to be pulled, flying behind her. "Don't let go!" he squealed.

With Tiny firmly in her grip, Roberta cried out, "I got you!" Hitting top speed, Roberta was consumed with fear, her confidence shattered.

Tiny, clinging to Roberta's paw as tightly as he could was terrified beyond words. All too frequently, he would glance back over his shoulder, afraid that the monstrous trees were reaching out in terrifying pursuit.

Hand in hand, they fled deeper into the threatening darkness. Almost blindly, Roberta led the way. Trying desperately to regain her sanity, she mumbled over and over: "Trees are beautiful. There is no curse. It's all in my head. Trees are beautiful."

Slowly, step by step, Roberta came back to a sense of reality. She eased up her pace, allowing Tiny to put his feet back on solid ground.

Still looking over his shoulder more than not, Tiny was relieved to see that they were still in one piece. Trying not to think of the trees, he turned to Roberta, who was now mumbling something about Mother Nature and the Great Spirit.

Regaining her composure was taking longer than usual, but her ears were no longer thumping. Her frightful feelings subdued, she turned to face Tiny, who was still tightly holding her hand. "Tiny, these trees are a gift of Nature. Trees are to be appreciated, not feared."

Tiny, his heart still beating hard, could only manage a shrug of his shoulders.

"Tiny, you and I have just broken the myth of the Dark Forest. There is no curse. It was nothing more than an empty and harmless rumor."

"Not so harmless if you asked me," said Tiny, with his little eyes expressing both relief and wonder.

"It's all how you look at life, Tiny. Some see the roses, while other see the thorns."

Hand in hand, and again moving forward together, Roberta raised her head up high and began to sing:

"Me and the Turtle
Overcame another hurdle
When in your heart there's a song
Where you know nothing can go wrong
Ho! Ho! Ho! Me and the Turtle
Overcame another hurdle."

Tiny's childlike face let go a big smile. He truly enjoyed hearing Roberta sing a happy song. But there were moments, way down deep, when he preferred to hear the sweet sounds of home.

Chapter 14

Together the two tiny travelers continued to tramp through the tall trees. "Thank you for not leaving me behind, Roberta. And for holding my hand. I was really scared."

"That's what friends are for, Tiny. And for a moment, I, too, was terrified. I've learned a new respect of fear. First with that feline freak. And now with this Dark Forest."

"I feel better knowing I wasn't the only one afraid."

"You look better, too. Now, let's talk less and make some real progress. Okay?"

"I think we already have."

Roberta gave Tiny a second look. "Tiny, I do like your spunk."

Tiny beamed. "And I do like compliments."

"Tiny," she began, shifting back to that familiar, serious tone, "I do need time for some quiet thinking."

"How strange," Tiny thought, scratching his head. He couldn't remember Roberta ever needing quiet time before. Once again, he wondered if there was something wrong.

With one of them wearing a worried look, the two companions moved deeper into the Dark Forest.

After what seemed to be a long time, a squeaky voice broke the eerie silence. "We seem to be going in circles. Are we lost?"

Roberta, trying hard to maintain her composure, directed Tiny to a gradual stop. Without responding, she methodically gazed over their surroundings, trying to determine their whereabouts.

Meanwhile, Tiny's fear became greater than his patience, and he just couldn't wait any longer for Roberta to complete her survey. Almost looking in every direction at once, he asked again, but this time a little louder. "Are we lost?"

"Yes and no," she answered calmly.

"What do you mean by that?" said Tiny, fearing the worst.

"I don't know where we are - - - exactly. But I know where we're going." Then, in an effort to reassure Tiny, she said, "I'm sorry for getting us into this, er, situation. But we are not lost."

Tiny was touched, but not nearly convinced. Roberta sensed this and reasserted, "I'll find our way out."

"We're going home?" Tiny blurted hopefully.

Roberta realized too late that Tiny had misunderstood her. If she was to help him overcome his fear, she would need to choose her words more carefully. "No, we're not going back," she said firmly. "My Mom told me if I wanted to bring about changes in this uncivilized, lawless kingdom, I would need to go forward. And that's what we are going to do. And I will find the Great Cyrus. Of that, I have no doubt. Trust me."

"I do trust you, I guess. But I know that I'm lost. How do you know which way to go?"

Quicker than a star's blink, Roberta spun her head completely around, this time from right to left.

Tiny, wide-eyed, exclaimed, "How does she do that?"

"Forward is the way," she declared, again pointing with one of her long ears.

"But Roberta, how do you know for sure?"

"Female intuition!" she replied emphatically.

"We're surrounded by trees and every way looks the same!"

Tiny was right, but Roberta remained undaunted. With her self-reliance fully restored, she commanded, "Let's go forward!"

Moving deeper into the shadowy gloom, there was a triumphant skip to her hop. "Tiny," she blared, "stick with me and you'll go far."

Tiny pouted. "I think you've taken me far enough already."

Not getting a reaction out of Roberta, Tiny was heard to mumble, "I knew this would happen. You've gotten us lost in this dark, ugly place.

We're going to starve before we get out of this endless mess. We'll never see home again."

Roberta put her soft paw around Tiny's shoulder. "Tiny, my troubled compadre, don't be discouraged. Together we'll find Cyrus the Great."

"I don't think so. It's the curse."

"No, no, Tiny. You and I have conquered that myth. And together we'll conquer the Dark Forest. Trust me."

With his growing doubts, Tiny shook his spotted head. "As far as we know, no one has ever made it through this cursed forest. Those who tried, vanished never to be seen again. Why do you think we can escape this ugly place?"

"Because I have the Great Spirit to guide me and you at my side."

"Oh," said Tiny, more surprised than relieved.

Roberta, seeing the puzzled expression on Tiny's face, went on to explain. "Tiny with you at my side, more than not, has kept me from losing my mind. You're slow but sure. And I do need your steadfastness."

"Oh," was all Tiny could say. But under these fearful conditions, he wasn't sure that Roberta was being completely honest.

"Yes, Tiny. You have taught me patience. Slow but steady stays the course. With your patience and my perseverance, we *will* conquer this Dark Forest."

Tiny, with a heavy sigh, took the time he needed to collect his thoughts, while Roberta waited quietly. "I like compliments, but this time I feel overwhelmed."

"Well, I meant every word I said, Tiny. And when I feel overwhelmed, I just turn to the Great Spirit, which I've been doing frequently of late."

"The Cheetah," ventured Tiny.

"That Cat and this forest," she acknowledged.

"I do feel a little better. Thank you, Roberta."

"You're welcome. That's what friends are for. And remember, with each step we're that much closer to the end of our journey. And together we will find the Great Cyrus."

Tiny nodded but kept his troubled thoughts to himself.

Although Roberta remained optimistic, the two companions soon found themselves deeper into the forest with no apparent way out. And with each step, Tiny became more convinced about one thing. Turning to Roberta, he grumbled, "I know we're lost and you don't."

"Tiny, you're learning to think for yourself, and that's a measure of your growth. Now, we need to learn how to agree to disagree without being disagreeable."

"Or grouchy," added Tiny.

"Or grouchy," she repeated. Then she heard the unexpected.

"Roberta, I need some quiet time to think."

Roberta flicked her long ears. "Er, okay, Tiny. Is there something disturbing you?"

"Yes, and that's why I need some time alone."

"Is there anything I can do?" she asked sincerely.

"No. Not this time," Tiny replied, looking quite somber. "Just lead the way and I'll be close behind you."

Completely flabbergasted, Roberta scratched her furry chin. She quietly moved on ahead, wondering what was going on with Tiny. "Maybe, since I now need him, he doesn't need me. Wouldn't that be a switch?"

Deep in thought, the troubled Roberta continued to lead the way. Close behind, Tiny was making his own progress. After going a considerable distance, or so it seemed, Roberta's long ears flicked to the tune of Tiny's singing:

> "Oh, we don't seem so smart
> We travel so far in the dark
> Ho. Ho. Ho. Me and the gallant Rabbit
> Need to stop our terrible habits."

Roberta glanced over her shoulder and caught Tiny's childlike grin. She shook her head, and her frown became a smile. "Tiny, I really do believe you enjoy playing with my mind."

"Whooo me?" he hooted with that familiar look of innocence.

"Yes, you," she replied good-naturedly. "And even though I don't always appreciate your playfulness, I do like your spunk!"

Tiny beamed. "And I do like compliments."

Together their laughter split the darkness as they ventured on side by side leaving home far behind.

Chapter 15

Roberta's long ears twitched. She took Tiny by his hand and picked up her pace. Then without any apparent reason, she stopped abruptly.

Tiny was completely mystified by her strange behavior. "What's wrong?" he squeaked. Then, anxiously he looked about to see if he could find something wrong.

Roberta scanned her surroundings, her ears still twitching. "My female intuition tells me to stop here."

"Well my tummy tells me it's past lunch time. I'm hungry!"

Roberta, letting go of Tiny's hand, put her paw to her lips. "Shhh. Listen." There was an unnatural stillness in the air. She turned and glanced about, this time more cautiously. But nothing was seen or heard that could explain her strange behavior.

Tiny was searching, too. But all he could see were trees, trees, and more trees. "Roberta, are we lost?"

"No," she replied just above a whisper. "Actually, I believe we are here."

"Here? Of course we're here. We're not over there!" snapped Tiny, pointing to a very large tree.

Roberta continued her search. When her eyes fell upon Tiny, she stopped. "You sound grouchy. Are you angry with me?"

Tiny looked up. When he spoke, his irritation was gone. "I'm sorry. I'm just hungry. And I always snap when I need something to eat."

"Me, too," she said, hoping it would help him feel better. "And your apology is accepted." Moving closer to Tiny, she said gently, "I'm sure

Cyrus the Great will have a few wholesome tidbits for you. Maybe, even a handful of wild blueberries."

"Well, I hope the Owl So Big is more than your figment of your imagination. I'm so hungry I could eat one of these ugly trees."

At that moment, food was far from Roberta's thoughts. "Tiny, I do believe we are close to the end of our journey."

"But I don't see anything, " he said, sounding very discouraged. "What makes you so sure?"

"Why, these trees, Tiny. They're the tallest trees I've ever seen. They must be the sign I've been searching for. And they're telling us that the Great Cyrus is near."

Tiny snapped again. "Well, I'm starving! If that old Bird is as smart as you say he is, he should be here right now with something good to eat!"

"Tiny! I'm surprised at you!" she admonished with her paw on her hip. "When we meet Cyrus the Great, we'll need to be on our best behavior and to show him our utmost respect."

Tiny lifted up his head and released a tired sigh. "For you, Roberta, I'll try to be good."

"I know you will, Tiny. Of that I have no doubt."

Tiny, however, had enough doubts for them both. But in an effort to please Roberta, he kept his troubled thoughts to himself.

Roberta nodded her approval. Then shifting her attention, she said softly, "There's something special about this place. I sense it."

"I hope you're right," replied Tiny, trying hard to be optimistic.

"That's the spunky Tiny I know. It pays to enjoy the honey without the Bees."

Tiny tilted his puzzled head, but before he could react, Roberta quickly stated, "The sooner we move on, the sooner we'll find Cyrus the Great. Just think we could be on the threshold of meeting the wisest Creature who has ever lived."

Tiny, with his fleeting eyes, strained to see beyond the trees. "It's so dark I can't see. Will you hold my hand?"

"That's what friends are for," she said affectionately. She reached out. Her paw was steady and Tiny could feel the firmness of her grip.

As they moved forward into the darkness, Roberta thought she saw something straight ahead. Her long ears thumping with excitement, she increased her speed. "Tiny, I see the light! I think we're coming to the end of the forest!"

With growing anticipation, she held Tiny's little hand ever so tight. Like a flash, she took off with one of her famous jack-rabbit starts. Moving with increasing speed, Tiny raised his feet off the ground, allowing Roberta to run as fast as she could.

"I'm holding on!" cheered Tiny. "This time it's fun!"

"I have you!" she blared, now moving faster with each graceful leap. Now at top speed, she was zigzagging and darting between mammoth trees, ducking low branches, and leaping over giant-sized roots. Then, without warning, she screeched to an abrupt stop.

Tiny, still holding fast to Roberta's paw, shifted his hind legs back on solid ground. "Oh, my," he blurted wide-eyed. "Where are we?"

Roberta was awe struck. They found themselves on the outer limits of a vast, circular clearing lined by a thousand trees or more. There in the center of the clearing, standing alone in all its splendor, was the tallest tree they had ever seen.

Tiny looked up and up and up, his mouth agape. The isolated tree was so commanding, even Tiny was impressed. For the moment, his thoughts of food were forgotten.

Roberta slowly shook her head. She couldn't believe her eyes. This mighty tree dwarfed the surrounding trees, they themselves gigantic in size. Its leafy branches of vibrant reds, yellows, and greens, reached upward towards the sky.

Roberta sighed deeply. "Tiny, this colossal tree is the sign I've been searching for. I should have known. The sign had to be something special. Something that would reflect the greatness of Cyrus the Great. And what could be more grand than this natural gift of Nature?"

Out from the cold, dark shadows, Roberta and Tiny were greeted by the warmth of the sun. Each step brought them closer to the tree in the center. They were now only three hundred feet from their destination. Or so Roberta believed.

"I just knew this was a special place," whispered Roberta, her eyes captivated by this noble tree before her. "It's awesome."

Chapter 16

"Tiny our journey is over. We did it! We have found the home of Cyrus the Great."

Tiny nodded. "It's such a tall tree. But I don't see the big Bird."

"I'm sure he'll be here soon. And Tiny, just look at that beautiful, blue sky. And to see my morning star again. Great Spirit! Thank you! Thank you for everything!"

Roberta opened her arms wide, then closed them as though in a warm embrace with the midday sun. Slowly, her gaze descended from the open sky to the tree so grand, its colorful leaves reflecting the sun's brilliant light. "The wonders of Nature are beyond words," she sighed.

There seemed to be a powerful force that drew Roberta ever closer to this towering tree. She was compelled to go alone since Tiny was again preoccupied with his own search.

As Roberta drew closer to the center, the vision before her became increasingly more compelling. With each step, her fascination grew, and her speed increased in measure.

Then, nearly half way into the circular clearing, Roberta stopped. Instinctively alarmed, she spun around, realizing too late, that she was in the open, completely vulnerable to danger. She remembered many times being told not to do the very thing she had just done. How could she have been so reckless? Roberta's first impulse was to rush back to the safety of the outlining trees. On the verge of doing just that, she took two quick steps, then stopped. "I mustn't panic," she said aloud, still angry with herself. "I need to collect my thoughts - - - and fast."

In a moment of stillness, that quiet, soft voice from deep within was heard: *"If you want to make a difference, you will need to go forward."*

Roberta turned to gaze once more at the tree that stood alone, now just over a hundred feet away from where she stood. Then over her shoulder, she looked back to the beckoning forest that offered her safety.

She took a deep breath, then moved forward, willing to risk everything to find the Great Cyrus. Her first step was the hardest. As one step followed the other, her conviction replaced old anxieties. Moving with increasing speed, she advanced closer to the tree of trees.

Now only thirty feet from her destination, Roberta came to a gradual stop. She was breathing hard, overwhelmed by what she saw. With her keen vision, she began to span the length of this splendid gift. Higher and higher, and still higher, and yet, even with her sharp vision, its uppermost point was clearly out of sight. Letting go a deep sigh, she whispered, "Do I dare imagine that this mighty tree extends to the sky and beyond?"

Roberta flicked her long ears to catch the vibrations of the wind singing through the bright-colored leaves that glistened high over her head. Within the serenity of the moment, she knew for certain that this magnificent tree was the sign to let her know that Cyrus the Great was near.

Roberta stepped back and gazed skyward. Fully stretching out her arms, she cried out "This is the most marvelous tree I've ever seen! It's TREE-MENDOUS!"

Chapter 17

Still standing alone, Roberta continued to reminisce on how she and Tiny overcame the challenge of the Dark Forest where others had failed. Even though a part of her, *deep down inside*, was resisting the urge, she just couldn't restrain herself. With a feeling of self-gratification, she proclaimed, "I'm sooome Rabbit!"

Roberta's long ears flicked. She was now aware of the soft approaching sounds of Tiny. He was rejoining her after a futile search for something to eat.

"Tiny, this is the sign I've been searching for. This is a major triumph for us both. So Tiny, cheer up and be happy!"

"Roberta, I wish I could, but I don't have the energy." With that, he slowly sat down.

"But Tiny! Just try to appreciate the beauty of this marvelous tree. Why, it's - - - it's incredible!"

Tiny blinked. With renewed interest, he got up and moved closer. "This tree is *edible?*"

Roberta shook her head. "No, no," she laughed. "You misunderstood me. You have food on your mind."

"Well," he grumbled, "I wish I had some food in my tummy where it belongs."

Roberta was too elated to be upset with Tiny's grouchiness. "Tiny we're here! You and I have achieved what no one else has done for over three hundred years!"

This time even the numbers didn't impress Tiny. "Roberta, we haven't accomplished anything. We're out in the middle of nowhere doing nothing." Tiny let go a heavy sigh. Then turning to look in the direction of home, he flopped to the ground, bone tired.

With a caring eye, Roberta gave Tiny a close look. He seemed unhurt, but there was sadness in his little, green eyes. Not knowing what to do or say, she sat down beside him. Both were lost with their own thoughts, each one seeking their own consolation.

Had either one of them looked more closely, they most certainly would have made a discovery. But unknown to Roberta, and maybe indifferent to Tiny, there was something in the tree that they had overlooked. About thirty feet above their heads, there was a very large perch, partially hidden by the multicolored leaves.

Moments past by and the two companions became engulfed by an uneasy quiet, even the wind was now still.

But Roberta just couldn't leave well enough alone, and the silence was broken by her voice. "I wonder how the Great Cyrus will greet us. To say the least, it will be a momentous occasion. I just hope I'll be up to it. I do want to make a good impression."

"I wonder if that Owl Bird will have something for us to eat," Tiny snapped. "I'm hungry!"

"Tiny! Where is your proper respect?" she reprimanded, more disappointed than anything else. "Do you want the Great Cyrus to be angry with you?"

Tiny didn't like the sound of that. With a frightful look, he raised his head and said, "What could the Big Owl do to me if he did get angry?"

Roberta, with that grave demeanor, didn't waste any time telling him. "Don't you know that the Great Cyrus is one of the most powerful predators of the jungle?"

Tiny shook his head timidly. Poor Tiny. He wasn't nearly prepared to hear more, but Roberta was just beginning her grim tale. "Why, he has long, sharp claws, a hooked beak, and he flies as swift as the wind. He can stoop down from the sky, yank you up by the back of your neck, take off for the clouds, then drop you over a pile of hard rocks! SPLAT!" she added with her arms fully extended, dramatizing one big, gory splash.

Tiny trembled all over as though he had actually felt the fear of falling, and then being smashed by the rocks below.

Roberta could clearly see how deeply he was affected by her vivid description of brute force. "I'm sorry I had to be so graphic, but I did it for your own good. So now you know that the Great Cyrus can make for a vicious enemy. And vicious enemies you don't need."

If it had been Roberta's intention to impress her little friend, she had succeeded. Or so it appeared.

Down deep, Tiny was feeling terribly confused. When his disturbing thoughts were interrupted with Roberta still yakking about her mighty Great Owl, that was the final spark that ignited his long, pent up anger.

As though a dam had been broken, Tiny EXPLODED!!! "From what I've heard, that stuffy old Bird Brain is nothing special, no better than any other Creature! He's a nobody living nowhere!"

Stunned, Roberta jerked back her head. Caught totally unaware, it was taking her longer to regain her composure. By the time she was ready to reprimand Tiny, her thoughts were sharply interrupted.

"And what's more!" Tiny blasted, "Owls hoot and screech all night long keeping their neighbors awake! Then they have the nerve to sleep away the whole day doing nothing!"

Roberta was completely dumfounded. And for the first time in her life, she was speechless.

But Tiny was only getting started. "And further more," he cried out, "their empty, feathered heads are much too big for their fat little bodies. Which I might add, they get by preying on helpless Creatures like Mice, Rats, and maybe from time to time, a cottontail Bunny for dessert!"

Roberta now stood erect, no longer in shock. Her long ears thumped angrily, which could only mean one thing: She was ready to put Tiny in his proper place. Never to be out shouted, she let loose. "How dare you say such horrible things like that. Who do you think you are? What if Cyrus the Great had heard you say all those terrible things about him? I have tried to warn you that he is a predator with keen hearing, to say nothing about his short temper and long, sharp claws. You're as stupid and shallow as your empty shell!"

During Roberta's tirade, Tiny surprised himself by standing his ground. There were moments when he was consumed by a powerful, instinctive urge to withdraw into his shell. But he had made up his mind not to give in.

By the look on Roberta's face, she was more surprised than Tiny that her heated words had not sent him cringing into his shell. "Maybe I'm losing my touch," she thought. "Well, I'll just make sure my words penetrate that thick skin of his. This time I won't hold anything back."

Determine to do just that, Roberta stared down at Tiny, and for one moment their eyes held fast. Tiny stood firm with no intention of darting into his shell. He was ready for anything that she might do.

With her paws on her hips, Roberta glared. But her anger never came. Thoughts were rushing through her mind faster than she could react.

Tiny, holding his head high, was troubled by his own feelings. "I don't like being angry. Now she's glaring down at me. Well, that's just too bad for her. But what do I do now?"

Roberta, now holding back her anger, wasn't quite sure what to do, either. But she took the first step. "Tiny, what am I doing? Friends don't shout at each other. I don't know what came over me."

"Neither do I." replied Tiny, his heart still beating fast. "I lost it." (Although at the time, Tiny didn't know he had actually found *it.)*

Roberta moved in closer. When she spoke, her voice was still shaken. "I'm truly sorry for all those terrible things I said about you. I didn't mean a word of it."

"I'm sorry, too. I don't like being angry. It hurts. And it's no fun."

"As you know all too well," she admitted, "I've blown up a number of times. I thought I had gained control of my temper. It seems I'll need to try much harder."

"Your anger and my pouting," said Tiny with a heavy sigh.

Roberta, with her soft paw, touched Tiny affectionately. "We need to always remember that friends don't bring pain to their friends."

"Roberta, you had little to do with my pain, because I remembered that you told me that words can't hurt me."

"That may be true," she said with her own heavy sigh. "But that does not excuse my behavior. During my tirade, I wasn't thinking of your feelings, only my own. My intent was to get back at you. But I know deep down I would never hurt you."

Tiny nodded. "I don't want to hurt you, Roberta or anyone."

"Especially, the Great Cyrus," offered Roberta. "You must realize for your own good that you can't go around saying horrid things about him.

As I warned you, he has lethal claws and a vicious temper, even worse than mine. You don't need his anger. It could be fatal. Why at any moment the Great Cyrus could swoop down and carry you off to oblivion."

This time, Tiny didn't look one bit intimidated. "Roberta, I'm tired of being nowhere waiting for someone who doesn't even exist."

"But Tiny, Cyrus the Great does exist! He's real and very much alive!"

For a moment, Tiny wavered, then raised his head a little higher. "For sometime I've come to believe that the Big Owl is just your vivid imagination, or that figment you carry around with you. Be honest and tell me the truth that the old Bird is nothing more than an empty rumor or just one of your exaggerated stories you made up."

"Tiny, friends don't lie to their friends. I'm prone to exaggerate at times, but only to get my point across. And I will never lie to you. Trust me."

"Well, I'll trust you to take me home, right now. Or I'll go home alone."

Roberta's ears flicked. She took a long, close look at her little friend, not wanting to believe what she had just heard. Tiny, although tired and weary, appeared determined. "I do believe he means it this time," thought a troubled Roberta. "Being a real leader may be a cut above my ability. What should I do now?"

There was an uneasy stillness, but *deep down inside*, Roberta heard that soft, gentle voice. And then she knew. Roberta took a deep breath and turned to face Tiny. "Tiny, I'll take you home."

Tiny gave a silent sigh. "Thank you, Roberta. I can get lost in my own shell. I really do need your help for a safe journey home."

"That's what friends are for," she said kindly. "And now that I know the way, I'll be coming back."

"And now that we know there's no curse to haunt us," added Tiny, trying to be positive.

Roberta gave Tiny a reassuring touch with her paw. She turned to the majestic tree for one last look, then back to Tiny. "When you know the right thing to do, making choices becomes a lot easier. Tiny, let's go home."

"Good afternoon, Tiny and Roberta." The voice from the sky vibrated with authority.

Roberta and Tiny were completely overwhelmed, unable to respond. Since there was no reply, the vibrant voice continued: "My well-traveled guests, allow me to introduce myself. "I Am Cyrus."

Chapter 18

For a long moment, the name Cyrus was all Roberta could remember hearing. It vibrated over and over in her head. She went completely limp, with her long ears dropping lifeless against her flushed cheeks. Then as though both far and near she again heard her name being called.

"Roberta and Tiny, I welcome you. My home is your home."

Roberta was so deeply affected by the inescapable authority of the Great Owl's voice, that she just now noticed that Tiny had disappeared into his shell, trembling. She didn't like being left alone, not for one moment. But she didn't know what to do about it, either.

With no help from Tiny, Roberta calculated that the voice was coming somewhere from the tree. Too unnerved to face the Great Owl, she kept her eyes straight ahead. She took a deep breath, trying very hard not to show how unnerved she was. Although afraid she already knew the answer, she asked guardedly, "Did you hear what Tiny, er, ah, what was said about you?"

"Yes, Roberta, I did." The Great Owl's reply was both direct and pleasant, but Roberta failed to hear the gentleness, only the words - - - and the pounding of her own heart.

"I feared - - - I mean I thought as much," she replied, as her knees began to wobble.

That did it! Right then and there, Roberta decided to get a hold of herself. When she spoke, her voice was steady, but her eyes never left the trunk of the tree. "I've heard that you can hear a leaf falling from the far side of the forest. Is that true?" she asked, her voice one word from cracking.

The Great Owl chuckled lightly. "I, too, have heard that rumor. Allow me to say that it's a gross exaggeration. I do apologize for overhearing your conversation. But as you said, I do have keen hearing. It's a powerful gift, but like all gifts, it, too, has its drawbacks."

Roberta was torn between what she thought she should do and the uncertainty of what might happen if she did. Trying hard to think through her confusion, she decided she had to face the Great Owl. She took another deep breath, then forced herself to look up.

There he was, sitting nobly on his perch, his large, orange eyes reflecting the brilliance of the sun. Roberta was mesmerized.

Chapter 19

Cyrus the Great Horned Owl - - - his stature was striking. There was also an unmistakable softness in his eyes. But Roberta, with her anxious thoughts, failed to see it.

From where Roberta stood, the Great Owl appeared awesome. And for good reason. With his hooked beak, sharp, pointed claws, and large penetrating eyes, he was not a Creature to provoke.

Curiosity got the better of Tiny. He stuck out his head and took one quick look. When he saw the Owl's piercing eyes, he darted back into his shell. After all those horrible things he had said about the Great Bird, he was not only terribly embarrassed, he was also afraid that he might be punished.

Roberta was feeling vulnerable. To be in the presence of one so exalted, was eroding away her confidence. She so much wanted to appear composed, but the fear she might crumble at any moment was all consuming.

"Oh, no. Not now." she moaned under her breath. "My ears are beginning to twitch. Won't I ever learn to hide my feelings?"

"You have beautiful ears," offered Cyrus with a warm smile.

A self-conscious Roberta replied, "Thank you, Great Owl. My ears seem to have a mind all their own."

"I have a friend who says the same thing about his tail," he chuckled. "Roberta, please call me Cyrus," which Roberta, being so tense, forgot as quickly as she heard it.

With renewed concentration, Roberta was determined to regain her composure, which was taken much longer than usual. Her troubled thoughts were interrupted when she heard her name being called.

"Roberta, you and Tiny are the first ones from the other side of the forest who had the courage to make this journey in, hmmm, nearly three hundred years."

From deep within his shell, Tiny blinked as he repeated the numbers to himself.

"Of course that was before my time," Cyrus added with a disarming smile. "To see you and- - -" Cyrus paused as he shifted his attention to Tiny's shell. After a moment or two, he turned back to Roberta and started again. "To see you and Tiny safe and well is a delightful treat for these old eyes."

Roberta was slowly regaining her composure. She liked what she heard, and found the Great Owl's demeanor quite pleasant. But after all those dreadful things that Tiny had said about him, she wondered if the Great Owl could be trusted.

Cyrus could clearly see that the two companions were overwhelmed by his presence. Patiently he continued his cordial welcome. "It would add to my pleasure if you and Tiny would join me for lunch in my tree house. I have prepared some refreshments, and for dessert we'll have a dish of wild blueberries."

Tiny heard that soft and clear. Without any hesitation, he poked out his spotted head and said all in one hurried breath: "I'm Tiny and I would like very much to have lunch with you and anyone else who might happen to drop by."

"Sheer rudeness," thought Roberta. But before she could turn to face Tiny, Cyrus chuckled merrily. "Wonderful, Tiny. I appreciate your enthusiasm."

Tiny's blush was followed with a shy smile. "I like compliments."

At that moment, Roberta allowed her mind to run wild, thinking that the Great Owl was setting a trap to lure them up to his lair. "Who knows," she thought to herself, "with those lethal claws, we could be *his* lunch."

Cyrus remained patient and said pleasantly, "I understand your concern. So allow me to reassure you both that I would enjoy your friendship. My invitation for lunch will give us an opportunity to get to know each other.

The Great Owl appeared sincere and his voice was pleasing to the ear. That Tiny liked. But yet, Roberta had a persistent fear that she might do the wrong thing. Never before had she faced this kind of situation. Too much was happening too fast, even for Rapid Roberta. Or maybe it was too much to be expected of one so young.

"Be brave," she said to herself, her eyes now fixed on Tiny. "I made a promise to protect him, and I plan to keep it."

Roberta made her decision. She stood tall, lifted her head and peered directly into the gleaming eyes of Cyrus the Great. Neither Cyrus nor Roberta blinked.

Chapter 20

For Roberta, what seemed to be an agonizing moment held in time was merely a flick of a Butterfly's wing. Her stare was broken with the softly spoken words of Cyrus the Great. "Roberta, would you feel comfortable if I flew down to meet you?" Gazing down from his perch, his eyes were clear and there was a tenderness in their glow.

At that very moment, Roberta felt a calmness come over her. And she knew, without knowing why, that the Great Cyrus could be trusted. Regardless of what might happen, she was willing to move forward.

Tiny felt something, too. "I'm hungry!" he said in earnest. "I'm ready to eat!"

"Now, Tiny," she admonished with an even tone, "remember your manners."

Tiny, not wanting to be rude, replied that he would try his best.

"Thank you. We don't want to provoke the Great Owl."

"No way!" agreed Tiny, his little eyes dancing about. "I'll be good."

Roberta again nodded her approval. She then turned to the Great Owl with a softer face and politely said, "Cyrus the Great, Tiny and I would very much like to accept your hospitality, if it's not too late."

"Not at all," smiled Cyrus. "Your timing is perfect."

"Hospitality?" pouted a disappointed Tiny. "What about lunch?"

Roberta was both embarrassed and upset. This time she would be more firm with Tiny. But before she could say a word, a chuckle was heard from above. "Tiny and Roberta, I can well imagine how hungry you must be after your challenging journey."

No sooner said when Cyrus spread his five-foot wing span to capture the breeze. His gentle glide was deliberate, not as a means to demonstrate his silent grandeur, but to allow his two young guests the time they needed to feel at home. Realizing this, he landed in such a manner that would help them feel secure.

Tiny and Roberta had watched the Great Owl during his graceful descent, and were captivated by his quiet elegance.

Now standing nearby, but not too close, Cyrus was nearly twice the size of Roberta. The Owl's short, pointed ears, gleaming orange eyes and his thick plumage of grays and browns gave him a distinguished appearance without looking arrogant. Or as Tiny might have said, stuffy.

As Cyrus approached them, he moved with a carefree confidence, although it was quite obvious he looked more natural in flight than when walking.

Tiny giggled, even though he tried not to. Not wanting to offend the Great Owl or displease Roberta, he quickly put his hands over his mouth.

"I, too, find my waddle amusing," said Cyrus with a lighthearted chuckle. "To be sure, these bowed legs were not made for walking."

There followed a quiet pause. A serious Roberta saw this as an opportunity to tell the Great Cyrus about her Crusade and the need for his support.

During her presentation, Cyrus had listened intently, while Tiny was relieved that he didn't have to make a speech, too.

"You and Tiny have journeyed from the other side of the forest to make this occasion possible. For your courageous effort, I will do whatever I can for you and your cause. You realize that there are no guarantees what the other Animals might do. There could be some strong opposition to your proposal."

Roberta, feeling both relieved and excited, failed to hear his words of caution. Quickly she turned to get Tiny's response, but his eyes were fixed on the Great Owl, completely entranced.

Mildly disturbed, but not knowing why- - - exactly, Roberta maintained her composure. Shifting her attention, she said respectfully, "Thank you, Great Cyrus. With your support, my proposal has an excellent chance of success."

Tiny followed Roberta's example, but in his own shy, quiet way. He smiled and nodded his head politely.

Cyrus returned Tiny's smile with one of his own, then bowed his large, feathered head graciously. And though a word was not spoken, Tiny was feeling very special.

Roberta watched the Great Cyrus and Tiny share their quiet moment. Not wanting to be left out she interjected, "Will you really help me with my Crusade?"

Cyrus extended his attention so that they both could feel included. "Yes, Roberta. My purpose is to be of service and I welcome this opportunity to serve you and Tiny to the best of my ability."

Tiny, hearing his name thought he should respond in kind. "Thank you, Cyrus the Horn. Er, I mean Great Big Bird of - - - Whoops. Oh, I'm sorry," he mumbled, feeling very embarrassed. "I just can't remember all those names."

"That's quite all right, Tiny. And please call me Cyrus. The titles are much too formal and really unnecessary, especially for an old stuffy Bird like me," he chuckled good-naturedly.

Tiny gasped. He raised his hands to his mouth, blushing profusely. "Oh. I'm sorry for all those terrible things I said about you."

"Tiny, there's no need to apologize, for no harm was intended and no insult was received. Why, one of my friends called me an old, foul Bird." A playful grin appeared on his hard beak. "But the remark I still most enjoy was when I was described as being an old stuffed up nocturnal tree-sitter. That gave me a good belly laugh for some time, and I always enjoy sharing it with my friends."

Tiny tilted his head and said, "You mean when you're called terrible names, it *really* doesn't hurt you?"

"That's correct Tiny. A verbal attack harms no one. It's a wonder how many still believe otherwise. And because they do, they become victims of self-inflicted pain."

"Roberta told me that words don't hurt," offered Tiny, with his expressive eyes in full motion. "But sometimes I forget."

"Roberta is absolutely correct," affirmed Cyrus. "When others call me names, I use their behavior as a reminder that I need to grow, and that I am no better than anyone else. Being called names, no matter how apparently vicious or *foul*," he added with a chuckle, "can be used as a humbling experience."

As Roberta looked on, she was feeling a bit neglected, but not knowing why- - exactly. But she perked up when she heard Cyrus say, "My well-traveled guests, shall we *rise* to the occasion and have lunch in my tree house?" Even Roberta could say yes to that, but not as fast, nor as enthusiastically as Tiny.

For the second time, Tiny and Roberta had missed Cyrus' play on words. And it wasn't until Roberta detected his humorous grin that she responded with a belated, but guarded smile.

Cyrus shrugged his feathered shoulders, then flashed Roberta a playful wink. "One of my weaknesses is that I enjoy being punny."

Before Roberta could respond, Tiny was already straining his neck skyward. "Cyrus, how high is your tree house, anyway? It's sooo high, it's out of sight."

"My, oh, my. You are perceptive. Tiny, from where we stand going straight up, my home is approximately one mile high."

"Wow!" blurted Tiny, his eyes expanding to the size of green grapes. "That's for me!"

Cyrus gently put his powerful wings on their shoulders, but only for a moment. "At that height, no matter which way you look, the view is divine."

That suited Roberta just fine, as she mused with anticipation. Tiny however, thinking Cyrus had said *dine*, cried out, "I'm starved! Let's go for it!"

Roberta flicked her long ears. When she whirled around to firmly remind Tiny of his manners, he stepped back, wondering what he had done wrong to bring about her displeasure. But again, before she could say a word, Cyrus, apparently unaffected by their behavior, said cheerfully, "My special guests, *let's go for it!*"

Tiny, now bursting with excitement, was the first to choose a wing. He could hardly wait. Roberta was also excited, and not to be outdone, hopped on the open wing.

When satisfied that Tiny and Roberta were safely secured for their first flight, Cyrus hooted, "Here we go!" And off they went. Up and up and up, with the cool wind caressing their faces, the young companions felt the exhilaration of flying.

"Wheee!" cheered Tiny. " This is fun!"

As they ascended higher and higher into the endless blue, a queasy Roberta glanced down at the spinning Earth below. "I just remembered something."

"What's that?" Tiny shouted above the whirling wind.

"I don't like high places," she moaned, turning several shades of green.

"Wow! You look like me!" teased Tiny playfully.

"Anything higher than a hole in the ground makes me dizzy."

"Roberta, try looking skyward," offered Cyrus. "If you observe the total view, you will feel better."

Before them, as they soared higher with the wind, the afternoon sun seemed to change colors, from yellow to orange to red. The purple-green mountains off in the distance reflected their silent strength. Beyond, there was the timeless ocean embracing the shore's sparkling sands.

Looking up and about, Roberta was captivated by the natural splendor that came into view. "The world we live in is truly a beautiful place," she sighed, forgetting for the moment her fear of heights."

"Woo Hoo!" Tiny cheered again. "Flying is for me. I've never been so high or moved so fast."

Cyrus smiled. Tiny's childlike enthusiasm touched his own youthful spirit. Spontaneously, he joined Tiny's joyful laughter.

Lost in her own world, Roberta observed the breathtaking view as it expanded out before her. Cyrus chose not to disturb her, not even with a soft whisper or with a gentle touch.

Flying on a wing, soaring high above the clouds was an exhilaration experience that the two young navigators would long remember.

Chapter 21

Higher and higher they flew. Tiny shouting with glee, enjoying the thrill of flying, while Roberta was content to quietly observe the natural beauty that extended in every direction as far as the eye could see.

From far below, what was once lost in the sky, now emerge into something real. There it stood with its cone-shaped pinnacle, reaching up into the sky. "Look!" shouted Tiny. "An upside down cone, like a giant finger pointing the way!"

Cyrus smiled affectionately. "Tiny, you are perceptive. What you say may be truer than we realize."

Tiny beamed. "I like compliments." A somber Roberta could only shake her head.

With each powerful sweep of his wings, more of the tree house came into view until it could be clearly seen.

"There it is!" cheered Tiny. "The sky home!"

Delighted with Tiny's exuberance, Cyrus smiled to himself. Within moments, he adjusted his wings to reduce his speed. There followed a smooth landing, much to the relief of Roberta, but much too soon for Tiny.

Their first flight was over, and each had gained from their own unique experience. Before going inside, they stood on the open balcony that was shaped like a half-moon. Tiny, still excited, spouted, "Your sky home is- - -oops! I mean your tree house is neat."

"Thank you," Cyrus replied. Then thoughtfully, "Sky Home. Hmmm, I like the sound of it. Tiny, from now on, that shall be the name of my home."

The sparkle in Tiny's eyes revealed his inner joy. Roberta turned from the view, but said nothing. She did admit to herself, though, that Sky Home did sound somewhat appropriate. Observing Cyrus and Tiny together, she couldn't help but notice their emerging friendship.

"Flying is fun!" grinned Tiny. "Let's do it again!"

Cyrus reached over and touched Tiny's shoulder. "Tiny, that will be my pleasure."

Tiny beamed as never before. Chills went up his back just like the time when he received his new name.

With increasing self-doubts, Roberta stood silently by. Her thoughts were interrupted when she heard Cyrus inviting them into his home.

Inside, Tiny and Roberta found Cyrus' mile high cabin to be comfortable. By most standards it was modest, fairly neat, and most assuredly, lived in.

For Tiny, whose only experience was living in a shell, the Sky Home looked like a royal palace. "Cyrus, your home is fit for a king."

With a light chuckle, Cyrus replied, "Tiny, I'm far from being a king, nor do I wish to be - - - "

"Never?" interrupted Roberta, breaking her long silence and one of her own rules. "From my way of thinking, having the authority of a king would be a worthy achievement."

With innocent curiosity, a belated never came from Tiny.

Cyrus was about to respond, but since Roberta was again distracted by the view, he turned to Tiny. "Never is a long time. For now, and the foreseeable future, my joy is enhanced by serving others." Cyrus paused momentarily to observe Roberta, who was now standing by the balcony.

When Cyrus returned to Tiny, he was the only one listening. That didn't seem to matter, as he continued to share his thoughts to his audience of one. "Each day I thank our Great Spirit for giving me the opportunity to serve the Animals of our kingdom. And that's just one reason why I have no need to be king. To obtain self-control is a worthy achievement, and far more important than the need to control others. Besides," he continued with a self-effacing smile, "for me, learning self- control is a full time job."

Neither Tiny nor Roberta responded. Tiny just nodded, enjoying the undivided attention that was so freely given, while Roberta remained standing alone.

"It's beautiful. Simply beautiful," she whispered.

"Yes, Roberta. Nature is a gift to be appreciated." As Cyrus waddled across the circular floor to join her, there was a light giggle. Without turning to a blushing Tiny, Cyrus grinned, "Walk this way, Tiny."

Even though Tiny was inclined to take Cyrus' play on words literally, he was content, for the moment, to stay where he was.

High overhead, pink clouds drifted by. "It's truly a marvelous view," she sighed.

"Yes, Roberta. What the Great Spirit has created for us to enjoy is inspirational. I would willingly give up my Sky Home for a rustic shack. But a view of Nature, I would hope would be mine forever."

Roberta nodded her agreement, and Cyrus knew she understood. Without another word, they shared their interlude together.

"When do we eat?" squealed Tiny, his anxious voice splitting the silence.

A startled Roberta flicked her long ears. Her special moment broken, she spun around ready to vent her displeasure. But once again that was not what Tiny heard.

"Thank you, Tiny," Cyrus said politely. "I invite you and Roberta for lunch, and what do I do, but become so involved that I forget my social etiquette and your refreshments."

Roberta, her ears still twitching, stood dumfounded. To hear Cyrus apologize to Tiny, after he had been so rude, was more than she could comprehend. "If anyone needs to apologize," she said to herself, "it should be that tiny nuisance."

Again her thoughts were broken when she heard Cyrus say, "I'll quickly redeem myself by serving lunch without further delay."

"All right!" cheered Tiny, who promptly accepted Cyrus' open invitation. When he reached the entranceway, Cyrus bowed playfully, and with the sweep of his wing, he ushered Tiny into the kitchen.

Roberta watched them leave the room. Feeling dejected, she stood off by herself, not at all understanding Cyrus' behavior with Tiny.

Chapter 22

Out on the kitchen's open balcony, the three of them sat around a circular table of oak. After what seemed like a long time, with only her own painful thoughts for company, did Roberta decide to join them.

At home, under similar circumstances, her Pop would have coaxed her to join the family. She waited for Cyrus to do just that, but it was as though she wasn't even there. Or even worse - - - a nobody.

When Roberta eventually did join them, Tiny gave her a quick, friendly nod. He then proceeded to bite into a slice of red apple, while Cyrus stood up and greeted her with a cordial bow. Nothing was said of her belated arrival, which relieved her of one concern, but was quickly replaced with another.

Roberta was now wondering had she not joined them, would Cyrus have let her remain alone, and if so, for how long? When she asked, Cyrus responded, with a disarming smile, that her question provided *food for thought*, but now was the time to nourish their bodies.

Roberta hesitated, prepared to pursue the matter, but then accepted a serving of carrots and dark green spinach. She found them to her liking. They were fresh and crisp. She had forgotten how hungry she was.

It was a scrumptious meal, which they all enjoyed. Especially Tiny, whose greatest joy came when he had an ample serving of his favorite dessert. His delight was also enhanced when he discovered that with their seating arrangement, everyone was sitting in the middle at the same time. When he shared his discovery, Roberta reacted with a smirk. Cyrus, without saying a word, reached over and gave Tiny a gentle squeeze. Tiny lifted up his head, grinning and blushing at the same time.

Roberta, feeling despondent, tried hard not to show it. She also had an uneasy feeling that she wasn't fooling Cyrus for one moment.

Now that his tummy was full, Tiny felt much better. Turning to Cyrus, he said joyfully, "Eating in the round is fun!"

Roberta flicked her long ears. "I do believe that you would find eating on your hard head enjoyable," she teased with an obvious tone of sarcasm.

An awkward stillness followed. Tiny, shifting his attention from Roberta to Cyrus, rolled up his little eyes and pouted. It was a big scene, but Cyrus remained unruffled. (No pun indented.) The gentle expression on his face seemed to say that there was no need to feel hurt.

"My well-traveled guests," offered Cyrus, breaking the silence, "thank you both for joining me for our first meal together. I enjoy my meals even more when I have friends with whom to share. It was DE-LIGHT-FUL!"

This time, Tiny picked up on Cyrus' playfulness and chimed in. "Even the green greens were greener and the blueberries bluer!"

A dismayed Roberta flicked her ears again, while Cyrus replied, "Tiny, I do enjoy your spirit and your *taste* for living."

Again missing his pun, Roberta turned to Tiny and teased sarcastically, "Only when it comes to eating."

This time, Tiny ignored both Roberta and her unkind remark. "Thank you, Cyrus. I like compliments."

"You're welcome," returned Cyrus, giving Tiny a tender caress. "Well, my friends, the abundance that the Great Spirit provides has given us the opportunity to share the *fruits* of Nature.

This time Roberta heard his play on words, and catching his eye, she slowly shook her head with a mock frown.

With a childlike smile, Cyrus shared, "I trust you will excuse an old Owl with his feeble attempts with puns. It's just one of my many habits that I haven't yet conquered." Then, turning to include his two young guests, he stood up and said, "Now that lunch is over, it's time for me to clean up."

"I'll help!" volunteered Tiny, as he dropped to the hardwood floor with a clank.

Still upset, Roberta glanced over to Tiny, then offered halfheartedly, "I can help."

Choosing to ignore Roberta's sullen tone, Cyrus responded, "Splendid! I can use all the help I can get. Let's go for it!"

A somber Roberta remained at the table alone, her head filled with disturbing thoughts. And not knowing why - - - exactly. She felt as empty as a discarded seashell.

Chapter 23

Roberta, still sitting alone, was struggling to understand what was happening. With a throbbing headache and unhappy with herself, the time seemed to drag slowly by. Now, quietly letting go, she heard that kind, gentle voice from deep down inside: "*Roberta, remember the words of your Mom.*"

Roberta brought her paws to her flushed cheeks. "I've been living backwards, while Tiny has been moving forward. Instead of thinking where would Tiny be without me, where would I be without him? Most likely I would be home in a hole washing twenty-two long ears. Mom, I'm moving forward!"

She then took a deep breath to regain her composure. Once again, it was taking a little longer than usual.

When Roberta bounced into the kitchen, Tiny and Cyrus were nearly done with the cleanup. Even so, they were quick to accept her offer to help. When the chores were completed, they moved into the living room and took their places at another circular table, this one of mahogany.

Tiny was elated. He liked sitting in the middle. But even more, he had someone who listened while he talked. To have Tiny share his thoughts, all it took was an encouraging nod or a smile, and he would flip from one topic to another. Before now, Tiny hadn't realized that he, too, had something worthwhile to say. With his eyes doing their dance, he was now reliving his flying adventure.

For the moment, Roberta was content just to sit and listen. When Tiny paused to catch his breath, Cyrus responded with a spontaneous hoot.

Immediately, Tiny tried one of his own, but all he got was a loud squeal. This prompted a round of laughter.

"Good try, Tiny," assured Roberta, her need to tease now under control. Then, catching Cyrus' attention, she turned serious and asked, "Do you ever get lonely way up here all by yourself?"

"That's a good question, Roberta." Gently, he reached his wings around their shoulders, which prompted Tiny to say, "Now you're in the middle!" Cyrus returned Tiny's smile, then to Roberta, he replied, "I do spend much of my time alone, but I seldom if ever feel lonely."

"How come?" asked Roberta.

Tiny, with that inquisitive look in his eyes, came up with the same question, but a moment or two after Roberta's.

Cyrus gave his two young guests an affectionate squeeze. "When I am alone and need reassurance, I take time to observe the total view. At that moment, allowing myself to let go of my thoughts, I feel an inner oneness with the wonders of Nature. Over the years, I have learned to enjoy my solitude. It gives me an opportunity to reflect and to offer my gratitude to our Great Spirit."

From across the table, Tiny and Roberta exchanged glances that revealed that they did not fully understand everything he had shared.

As Roberta tried to sort out her confusion, a light chuckle was heard. "It appears that I did not make myself clear. Someday, at the perfect time, you will both understand what I was trying to convey." Having said that, Cyrus lifted up his wings and placed them in his lap.

"But Cyrus," expressed Tiny, "when you're all alone, you have no one to play with. What do you do then?"

"Why, Tiny, we have the whole Universe to play with any time we choose."

"The Universe is a playmate!?" said Tiny with a look of wonder.

"What a novel idea, Tiny" smiled Cyrus. "To see the Universe as our playmate is quite perceptive."

Tiny beamed. "I like compliments."

Roberta, at that very moment, felt his soft feathered wing go around her shoulder, followed by a gentle caress. And even though Tiny had the other wing, she was feeling very special.

Cyrus' easy manner became solemn, but only momentarily. When he spoke, a soft smile appeared at the corners of his hard beak. "Dear ones, my renowned friend, The Elder, has been known to say, 'The higher, the fewer.'"

That, Tiny could understand. Or so he thought and said brightly, "You sure do live high up!"

Amused, Roberta slowly shuck her head, saying, "Nice try, Tiny."

With a gleam in his eye, Cyrus gave them both a playful squeeze.

Tiny let loose a big grin, while Roberta again turned serious. Now deep in thought, she was trying hard to understand all that Cyrus had shared. But the harder she tried, the more confused she became. Never willing to let things go, she felt a need to pursue the matter. But first, feeling closed in, she stood up to slip away from his wing. There was no resistance.

As Cyrus gently released her, he whispered, "Oneness."

She quickly crossed the floor to the balcony. Pushing aside her confusion for the moment, Roberta scanned the remote mountains that now reflected a purple hue from the late afternoon sun.

As Cyrus quietly observed her, he caressed Tiny with the tip of his wing.

Roberta, with a far away look in her eye, said softly, "How my parents would enjoy such a view." Then quicker than a bubble's burst, she spun her head completely around.

Tiny shook his head and blinked, while Cyrus blared with delight. "Hey! That's splendid!" He then rose to his feet, lifted his wings straight up and spun his feathered head completely around.

Tiny was both bedazzled and disappointed at the same time. He glanced from Roberta to Cyrus, then back again before fixing his bewildered eyes on Cyrus. Heads were spinning faster and faster. "How do you do that trick?" he squealed, feeling left out.

"The trick, as you call it," bellowed Cyrus between a series of head spins, it's due more to heredity than to any great talent."

Tiny heard, but what he saw reinforced his hurt feelings. "But I can't do it," he pouted. "My hard shell hinders me more than it helps me."

Cyrus, his head no longer spinning, turned to a very unhappy Tiny. "Nature has a mysterious and wondrous way of providing gifts to every living Creature. And with our natural gifts we also have natural shortcomings. The *trick* is to accept who we are. Self-acceptance is a key to living a joyful life."

Roberta, who had resumed her head spins, came to an abrupt stop. "Tiny, that's the answer to your question. *Acceptance* is the second step to learning. Now we both know."

Tiny barely nodded, and his pout remained. "Cyrus, you don't have any shortcomings. You're perfect."

Roberta agreed completely and gave Tiny a supportive glance. Then shifting her attention, she said with a half smile, "Cyrus, we got you now. Don't play modest with us. We know that you are honored for your wisdom and that you are perfect by any measure."

Amused by their naivete, Cyrus replied with that self-effacing smile. "I am far from being perfect. My word, if I were perfect, I most likely couldn't stand myself."

"But you seem perfect," countered Roberta, unwilling to believe what she had just heard.

Cyrus sighed. "I have unintentionally given you two the wrong impression. Yes indeed. Mercy. Mercy. I have lived a long life, and on my journey, I have discovered contentment. But like everyone, I have my share of imperfections and my lessons to learn."

Tiny blinked. "You have lessons?"

Roberta scratched her furry head in disbelief. "Cyrus, we don't see any flaws in you. All we see is your wisdom and your position of authority. You are everything I want to be."

Aware that they were taking him much too seriously, Cyrus put on a goofy grin. Then, with an exaggerated wail, he declared, "Before you and the whole Universe, I confess that, like all the other Creatures of our kingdom, there are many, many things I cannot do!"

A disillusioned Roberta slowly shook her head. "Now you're being silly."

"That may be true," Cyrus hooted spontaneously.

A sparkle of merriment appeared in Tiny's eyes, as he responded to the playfulness of Cyrus the Great. "What are they?" he said with his own squeaky hoot.

"My, oh, my. Where should I begin?" Cyrus replied with a chuckle. "Well, for one thing I can't carry my house with me wherever I go. Nor am I as sure-footed as you, Tiny."

Tiny blushed, then turned on a silly grin trying to look like Cyrus.

Cyrus tooted his approval, then gave Tiny another silly face to work on. Then just as quickly, he whirled around to face Roberta, saying, "And there's no way that I'll ever zigzag as fast as you, my friend. Or as in my case, waddle," he added with three more hoots.

Tiny raised his hand to cover his mouth, but he was too slow, allowing several giggles to escape through his fingers.

Roberta, still shaking her head, remained perplexed.

Cyrus gyrated over to Tiny and declared, "Nor will I ever be able to thump my ears together like Roberta. Mercy. Mercy."

Tiny shook his head. He then doubled over with laughter, watching Cyrus struggle through several facial contortions trying, without success, to thump his short, pointed ears.

Roberta just stood there with a bewildered look on her face. She couldn't understand how one so wise and dignified could now be acting so childish and undignified. "Cyrus, be serious," she implored. "You're wise beyond compare and you hold a position of honor. You can do anything you really want to do. Isn't that true?"

Cyrus chose not to respond directly to her question. Instead, that playful grin reappeared. "If you think my waddle is amusing, imagine the frightful sight I would make trying to swim."

Allowing time for that image to sink in, Cyrus made a series of exaggerated strokes with his outstretched wings, creating the effect that he was struggling to swim upstream. "On second thought," he hooted, now demonstrating an awkward backstroke, "you may never see me soaking wet. Now, if I could walk as graceful as Tiny swims, that would be poetry in motion. Huh, Tiny?"

Tiny, blushing and laughing, responded loudly, "I guess so."

"Mercy. Mercy. Swimming my feathered body can do without. My good friends, thank you very much. Yep, you two will just have to fantasize the forlorn spectacle I would make, wet feathers and all."

Tiny did just that, and his giggles blended with Cyrus' hearty laughter.

Roberta was not amused, and her disappointment could be clearly heard by the tone of her voice. "But Cyrus, there are many things you can do and so many things I can't do."

"One does not have to do everything to be successful or content," offered Cyrus . "Just be yourself, learn what you can, and don't worry over the things you cannot do."

"It all seems so hopeless," argued Roberta. "I have so much to learn."

"Hopelessness is just a state of mind," replied Cyrus reassuringly. "You are young and yet you are learning a great deal: friendship, courage, caring - - - "

"But how can I learn all that you know?" she interrupted.

"You show an eagerness to learn. That is proper and wise. But it is also wise to know that no one can learn everything in one lifetime. So my young and aspiring friends," Cyrus concluded with that gleam in his eye, "save some lessons for next time."

Tiny was now beyond caring. Still trying to get off a good sounding hoot, he was having fun and he was ready for more.

Unlike Tiny, Roberta could feel her frustration build, and not enjoying it for one moment. "Next time!?" she blurted. "What next time?"

"Roberta, I do believe you want to learn everything all at once. And one thing I have learned is not to take life or myself too seriously. We are here to learn what we can, being who we are."

Following a moment of reflection, Cyrus continued. "And as we live and learn, we come to appreciate that what we experience occurs at the perfect time. Life allows time for growing, working, singing, crying, dancing, and - - -" Cyrus paused. Turning to Tiny, he shared with a childlike wink, "And a time to laugh and play."

Tiny nodded with a very big grin.

But Roberta was far from being convinced, and her long face revealed a serious frown.

Undaunted by Roberta's despondence, Cyrus hooted, "Sooo children of the Universe, as you live your great adventure and continue on your journey, realize that you can't learn everything in one lifetime."

"Like swimming!?" Tiny spouted with a loud squeaky hoot.

Spontaneously, Cyrus lifted his face toward the ceiling and bellowed with laughter. His whole body shook, feathers and all, while Tiny watched with pure enjoyment.

Roberta was still troubled by what she didn't understand. Not in the habit of giving up, she looked across the room to catch Cyrus' attention. "But what do you mean by next time?"

It was obvious that Roberta was still taking it all too seriously. So it occurred to Cyrus, it might be appropriate and fun to change the situation. His decision and performance were simultaneous.

The big Bird spun around, then deliberately took several waddles to the center of the floor. That alone drew giggles from Tiny. But Roberta just continued to stare as she tried to make sense out of what was sheer nonsense.

Cyrus realized he had a real challenge with Roberta. But the fun was just beginning, and she could not possibly know what was about to come her way.

To begin his charade, Cyrus quickly spun his head completely around, sending a very silly grin to Tiny who was more than willing to play. Now gazing straight ahead, he blared, “Watch closely. Can either one of you do this?”

Tiny, who was already under Cyrus’ magical spell, yelled out, “Are you going to show us a new trick?”

“All right! A trick it shall be!” resounded Cyrus, this time a little louder. Then quicker than a Monkey’s chatter, he flashed a wink the size of a large grapefruit to Tiny, who doubled over with laughter.

For the moment, Cyrus was giving his full attention to Tiny. He was aware of Roberta’s unyielding resistance to let go. But her time would come, of that there was no doubt.

Cyrus lifted his wings high over his head and began to whirl around the circular room faster and faster, hooting and screeching as he did. As stout as he was, it was surprising to see him move so gracefully.

As Cyrus continued his antics, Roberta stood off, slowly shaking her head. But Tiny, dizzy from watching the old Owl’s gyrations, was delighted and his laughter filled the room.

‘Round-and-‘round-and-‘round Cyrus went, twirling as he did. With each turn around the room, his spinning circles became smaller and tighter until he reached the center. There he stopped abruptly, balancing on his toes. He stood motionless, and even that appeared exaggerated. Then with his bulging eyes, he hooted:

“KOSMOS!”

A deeply confused Roberta rushed her paws to cover her ears, while Tiny added his own loud hoots, sounding more like Cyrus. And to the delight of one, more merriment was sure to come.

Now his large eyes flashing, Cyrus tooted, "Watch closely, because now you see it, now you don't." And like the last flicker of a shooting star, his large, feathered- head vanished.

Tiny was spellbound and his eyes expanded to the size of giant, green grapes. Before he could close his gaping mouth, Cyrus' head popped up, flashing eyes and all.

Roberta remained detached, not wanting any part of his foolishness. When Cyrus began to hoot and whistle, she again raised her paws to cover her ears. Convinced that Cyrus was lost in his own madness, she moved to the far side of the room.

Far from being discouraged by her aloofness, Cyrus whirled around the room again and again, his large head dipping out of sight, only to pop back onto his feathered shoulders. On occasion, his head would surprisingly pop up backwards, causing Tiny to laugh so hard that he doubled over again.

Faster and faster Cyrus twirled, lifting his wings up toward the ceiling. Then, suddenly he stopped dead center. Tiny, watching his every move, fell out of his chair and hit the wooden floor with a loud CLANK. Picking himself up, he gazed into Cyrus' glowing eyes, now no longer just a spectator. What Tiny accepted as fun and play, Roberta judged as childish and demeaning.

Tiny, his playful spirit touched by the mystical spell of Cyrus, zipped into his shell. "Look at me!" he shouted as his head popped up. Zip! "Look now!" he yelled from inside his shell. "I'm all gone." Zap! Tiny reappeared, his tail wagging with joy. "I'm all here again!" he cheered. "I'm a miracle!"

"Fantastic!" wailed Cyrus, as Tiny zipped in and out of his shell. "And yes, Tiny, I do believe you are a miracle!" Their laughter rang out, loud and clear. Together they scooted, skipped and danced, as Tiny added his own hoots sounding just like Cyrus.

Roberta once again rushed her paws over her ears. She was now completely disillusioned. The entire spectacle looked utterly ridiculous. She could forgive Tiny, but there was no excuse for Cyrus the Great who was old enough to know better.

"Nonsense," Roberta surmised, as she continued to judge Cyrus from a safe distance. "Utter nonsense! I do believe he has gone totally out of his mind." In her eyes, Cyrus was behaving just like an overgrown child. (Actually, without knowing it, Roberta was Right On.)

Then quite by accident, or so it seemed, Roberta was caught by one of those flashing "grapefruit" winks. She snapped her head resisting a deep urge to let go. But, oh so slowly there appeared a faint hint of a reluctant smile, followed by a soundless titter, a snicker, a giggle or two. And then a soft laugh.

Caught off guard by a second flashing wink, Roberta's childlike spirit was aroused. Then quicker than a Flea can hop, set free.

Roberta pirouetted across the floor, her long ears thumping with ecstasy. Her senses amplified, her merry laughter merged with the medley created by an old, crafty Owl and a fun inspired, tiny Turtle.

Cyrus greeted Roberta openly, his large, orange eyes glowing brightly.

Tiny zipping in and out of his shell, was overjoyed to see Roberta enter their magical world of play.

Following Cyrus' lead, they joined together and formed a circle in the center of the room. Together they danced 'round-and-'round-and-'round, joyfully lost in the enchanted space they had created.

For that magic moment the threesome was delightfully
OUTRAGEOUS!

Chapter 24

The golden sun was now high above the clouds turning the western sky into a brilliant glow of reds and yellows. During their moment of play, thoughts of time had faded in and out for Roberta. For Tiny, there was no time, just an exhilarating, magical space of pure joy.

Roberta could admit to herself that she found the experience enjoyable. And at times, in some strange way, uplifting. Unable to make sense of it for the moment, and with other matters now occupying her thoughts, she was ready to take another step forward. With full decorum, Roberta turned to Cyrus and began her formal request.

Cyrus listened politely. He was amused by her formality, but said nothing, accepting her just as she was. He then invited his two young friends into his den.

Upon entering the circular room, it finally occurred to Tiny that the entire Sky Home was made in the round. "No wonder I'm dizzy," he grinned.

Cyrus responded with a wink while Roberta chose to ignore Tiny's remark. Her only thought was to get on with the proceedings. She looked very serious.

The den was tidy and comfortable, but Roberta was too preoccupied to have noticed. And maybe a little apprehensive. This was her big moment and she so wanted to do everything perfectly.

In his usual, gracious manner, Cyrus guided them to a table of ebony. There were three chairs. Roberta hesitated while Tiny took a seat without a second thought. It didn't seem to matter where they sat, since the wooden chairs were identical and the table was round.

Roberta sat up to the table with that solemn look in her eye. Tiny, sitting to her right, looked as though he didn't have a single care.

Cyrus spoke first. "Roberta, you may begin when you are ready."

Roberta tried to appear calm, but as soon as she heard her name, her ears began to twitch. "Oh no," she uttered to herself. "Not now. What will Cyrus think?" With total concentration, her ears stopped quivering. When she felt composed, which was taking a little longer than usual, she turned to face Cyrus. Then choosing her words carefully, she began in her most dignified voice: "Cyrus the Great Horned Owl, I am here to make an official request which requires your approval."

When Roberta paused to collect her thoughts, a personal request was offered. "Please call me Cyrus. Using my full name is unnecessary and much too formal among friends."

"And stuffy," chimed in Tiny, nodding his head in full agreement. He recalled all too well his embarrassment of trying to remember all those names let alone in their proper order.

Cyrus acknowledged Tiny with a brief nod, but from across the table, Roberta closed her eyes and slowly shook her head. She was in no mood to be interrupted. She was on edge, and she knew that any distraction could cause her to loose her concentration. And the last thing she wanted to do, was to appear foolish in the presence of Cyrus.

When Roberta shifted her attention back to Cyrus, he said reassuringly, "When you are ready, you may proceed with your request."

Taking her lead from Cyrus, she was feeling more at ease. "Cyrus, I hereby request that you call for a Grand Assembly to discuss a problem that involves the survival of our entire Jungle Kingdom."

"And all those who live in it," interjected Tiny.

Roberta flicked her long ears. With raised eyebrows, she glanced over to Tiny. It was her reminder that she was not to be interrupted again. Tiny got the message, and with a dejected pout, slumped back into his chair.

Cyrus waited patiently, and when Roberta was again ready, he said, "Roberta, please state the purpose of your request."

With increasing self-confidence, she began. "I request a Grand Assembly to bring all the Animals together for the purpose of creating a kingdom free of violence with peace and harmony for all."

"And free of starvation," offered Tiny, sounding very determined.

Roberta lowered her head. Turning to face Tiny, she said somberly, "Thank you, but I hadn't forgotten. Now, may I go on without any more interruptions?"

Tiny slouched and slipped deeper into his chair. "I was only trying to help," he mumbled.

"Tiny, you have helped," consoled Roberta. "But now it's time for you to listen." Turning back to Cyrus, she continued. "As I was saying, the purpose of the Grand Assembly is to establish a peaceful kingdom for everyone by eliminating violence - - -" Roberta stopped. She turned to Tiny, and with a casual nod, she added, "And starvation."

Tiny rolled up his little eyes and smiled with quiet satisfaction.

"Your request is well stated," confirmed Cyrus, "and worthy of having the Grand Assembly called into session."

Roberta let go a heavy sigh. Relieved and feeling a sense of pride, she turned to Tiny, but was disappointed when she saw a worried look. She had expected some kind of appreciation for what she had just accomplished. But no matter. To have the approval of the Great Cyrus was a major achievement. But once again, she was assuming too much, too soon. For when she guided her attention back to Cyrus, she was to receive her second disappointment.

There was a deliberate pause, for Cyrus wanted to emphasize the importance of the question he was prepared to ask. When he spoke, his voice was cordial but firm. "Roberta, when you say that *all* the Animals will be invited to the Grand Assemble, do you really mean everyone?"

Roberta could feel her ears begin to twitch.

Tiny, now squirming in his chair, was hoping she would just say yes. "I knew this would happen," he thought to himself. "She creates her own problems. Why does she have to be so stubborn?"

Roberta, deep in thought, took her time to carefully choose her words. Her ears no longer twitching, she stood up and stated, "Cyrus, I would like to make a request that all the Animals be invited with the exception of one. The Cheetah. And with your permission, I would like the opportunity to explain."

"By all means," Cyrus replied softly.

"The Cheetah is not just another Meat Eater," began Roberta, her voice steady and filled with conviction. "He has threatened to have my furry hide. His very words. That spotted Cat is out for vengeance. To attack just to satisfy his hate can never be justified. The other Meat Eaters eat out of need. There is always hope that they will see the advantage of accepting a kingdom free of violence. But there's no way that anyone can change the Cheetah. Since his heart is filled with hate, he is no longer worthy of being invited to the Grand Assembly."

Following a brief pause, Roberta stated firmly, "Based on the facts that I have presented, I see no reason to change my position." She then took her seat, feeling satisfied with her presentation, but was anxious to hear Cyrus' final decision.

Tiny looked befuddled. He had thought that the exclusion of the Cheetah was unfair and self-defeating. Now he wasn't so sure. Having a difficult time sitting still, he shifted his attention to Cyrus, who was prepared to address Roberta.

"Your discourse was well presented, Roberta. And what you say about the Cheetah is true. On one level, it would seem logical to exclude the Cheetah. On a higher level, however, all the Animals are one family. At the present time, we live under the dictum of tooth and claw. Under that law, there is no provision to exclude anyone from the Grand Assembly. If your request is worthy of being accepted, it must stand the challenge of including everyone without any exclusions. To make an exception based on fear or hate, would bring discredit to your worthy cause."

Roberta slowly nodded to let Cyrus know that she understood his position. But she was far from being subdued. When she spoke, her voice was steady, and there was also an obvious tone of urgency. "Cyrus, since the vote of the Grand Assembly must be unanimous, the Cheetah must be excluded. If not, my proposal is defeated before it's had a chance to succeed."

Tiny was now more confused than before. Not knowing what to say, he decided to say nothing.

"Seeing the situation from your point of view," reflected Cyrus, "I can appreciate your impasse." He paused, the gentleness in his voice never wavered. "If there is to be a Grand Assembly, every adult must be invited, including the Cheetah. There can and will be no exceptions. Roberta - - - we have come complete circle. The decision is yours."

From the corner of his eye, a nervous Tiny could see Roberta sitting motionless. "I wish I could help her," he thought. "But there's nothing I can do. I feel so helpless." He remembered the time when Roberta told him that there were those who were good at putting themselves into a *hole* of their own making. The thought brought him no comfort.

Cyrus sat reposed quietly waiting for Roberta to make her decision.

Roberta, thinking to herself, was deeply troubled by her own disturbing thoughts: "I'm in a dilemma. No matter what I decide I lose."

"*Not so*," said the soft, caring voice from deep within. *"Roberta, your choice is to quit or to continue to move forward."*

An uncommon stillness encircled the room. Cyrus continued to wait patiently.

Not so for Tiny, who was now a bundle of nerves, twisting and squirming in his chair.

Roberta stood up. Without saying a word, she gave Tiny a somber nod. She then turned to face Cyrus. Her voice was firm and even. "My Mom and Pop did not raise me to be a quitter. We're moving forward. The Cheetah is not to be excluded."

Cyrus, realizing Roberta's strong opposition to *include* the Cheetah, quietly accepted her choice of words.

Tiny was so excited, that he fell from his chair, hitting the hardwood floor with a loud CLANK. Standing upright, he cheered, "On with the Grand Assembly!"

"On with the Grand Assembly," repeated Roberta.

Cyrus smiled to himself. "How my two young friends have grown." Then as though speaking to a higher source, he said, "Thank you, so much."

Roberta let lose a loud sigh. "What a big relief. That's a heavy load off my shoulders."

"That's easy for you to say," ventured Tiny with a straight face. "I have to carry this heavy shell wherever I go and I never get any relief."

Cyrus raised his head, and his laughter circled the room. Roberta, with a faint smile said, "That was real clever, Tiny. Quite clever indeed."

Tiny looked on with innocent surprise.

"Tiny, let us hope that your burden will never be as heavy as the one Roberta has been carrying for some time."

Tiny nodded with a blushing grin. Then appearing nonchalant, he got back into his chair without a hitch.

"Today I've learned another lesson," shared Roberta.

"Yes I do believe we all have," affirmed Cyrus. "And before I give you both a big bear hug, let me quickly bring this session to a close."

When Cyrus had their attention, he began. "With the authority bestowed upon me, all the adult Animals of the Jungle Kingdom are invited to the Grand Assembly with the purpose of creating a peaceful kingdom for every living Creature by eliminating violence - - -"

"And starvation!" volunteered Tiny.

"And starvation!" repeated Roberta.

"And starvation!" offered Cyrus.

Cyrus then stood up and announced that the session was officially closed.

Tiny let loose a joyful, "Woo Hoo!" He then removed himself from his chair, this time without falling to the floor.

Standing together they all cheered, Tiny leading the way. The bear hugs quickly follow.

Chapter 25

It wasn't long before Roberta was feeling closed in. With her first move to break away from his embrace, she felt his powerful wings lift gently from her shoulders. Free, she left the den and hurried across the living room to the balcony. "Say! Look at this sunset. And those radiant colors."

"A sunset," offered Cyrus, as he and Tiny joined her, "is Nature's promise of a new beginning."

"That sounds more like a sunrise," corrected Roberta.

"Speaking precisely," Cyrus responded with that disarming smile, "you are correct. It was my feeble attempt to be poetic. Presuming that you'll accept my apology, we won't split any *hairs* over it."

Roberta slowly shook her head with a playful frown. "That Cyrus is your worst pun yet."

"I liked it." declared Tiny.

"Thank you, Tiny," he said with an exaggerated bow. "I needed that. Maybe I should stick to my poetry, such as it is."

Roberta, not knowing what to say, shrugged her shoulders, then gave her full attention to the setting sun.

As the flaming sun created its own poetry, they watched the glorious sky reflect a blend of yellows and reds.

Roberta gave Tiny a nudge and pointed, guiding her paw above the horizon. It was the elusive, green streak, extending itself, momentarily across the sky.

"Oh, my gosh!" uttered Tiny with a look of wonder..

Roberta placed her paw around Tiny's shoulder. "It's your first, and who knows, it may be a long time before we see it again."

Observing their drama unfold, Cyrus quietly reflected to himself: "Friendships can be as fleeting as the green streak, or as enduring as the eternal sun."

Not until the sun had disappeared from view, and twilight had its way, was another word spoken. Silence has its own special reward - - - and its own poetry.

As they leisurely prepared their dinner, Cyrus answered Roberta by saying, "Yes, that's true. Everyone has an Inner Voice. One only needs to be still and quietly listen."

"Will you teach me how to hear it?" asked Tiny, with a slight tilt of his head.

Cyrus smiled. "Tiny, there are many who *feel* their Inner Voice, rather than *hearing it*. When you truly want to sense it, you will."

Tiny beamed. And even more so when he heard Cyrus call out, "Dinner is ready."

For their evening meal, Cyrus had prepared a simple, but nutritious dinner. While dining under the stars, Roberta visualized their kingdom as peaceful as the evening sky.

Tiny, for the most part just ate, enjoying each morsel. He made sure his chair was next to Cyrus. Which wasn't hard to do, since every table in the Sky Home was round.

Roberta, fascinated by the shiny lights above, had no cause to compete for attention. She had a few questions she needed to ask Cyrus, but she could wait.

Cyrus observed his two young friends enjoying themselves. He knew that someday they would realize how much they had given him. Hearing a cheery voice, he responded fondly, "Yes, Tiny, you may have another serving of wild strawberries."

Tiny reached out for his second helping. "Blueberries were my favorite," he grinned. With that, his red lips helped another juicy strawberry to disappear.

Roberta glanced over to Tiny, shaking her furry head in mock astonishment. "Where does that little critter put all that food?" she thought, more amused than surprised. Then, in an effort to take away her own troubled thoughts, she turned back to gaze at a bright, starlit sky.

When Tiny completed his last strawberry, and not a bite sooner, he asked a question that Roberta might have considered inappropriate. “Cyrus,” began Tiny with a look of curiosity, “are you really one hundred and twenty-six years old?”

Before Roberta could react, Cyrus lifted up his head and bellowed with laughter. “Tiny, I only look that old. Actually, I just turned eighty-four last spring.”

With his eyes dancing about, Tiny repeated the numbers, then grinned. “That makes you younger than my great-grandmother.”

“Tiny, you are perceptive. And from time to time, I remind myself, that age is only a bunch of numbers. May we all stay young at heart. Now, would anyone care to have a few more strawberries?”

“No thank you,” Tiny chuckled. “My tummy is full.”

Roberta, too, was content and the strawberries, with the other leftovers, were carefully put away for another day.

Dinner long past and the chores completed, Roberta was once again struggling with a few fearful thoughts that just wouldn’t go away. Trying hard to relax, she continued to rock in one of the old, wooden rocking chairs. Her concentration was partially broken when a vibrant voice broke the silence.

“Tiny and I are going out to catch a shooting star. Would you care to join us?”

There was no immediate response. “Roberta, are you still with us?”

“Oh. I was just thinking.”

“You look like you’re carrying the whole kingdom on your shoulders. Would you care to share the load before we go for a midnight ride?”

“I’m worried about that vengeful Cheetah. It’s almost like a double curse. His vote and his threat to have me for lunch. What am I to do?”

“Roberta,” he said with a light touch in his voice, “since you asked, may I say that worrying won’t change the Cheetah’s disposition, nor will it change the future. Tomorrow is a moving target.”

After a pause, Cyrus continued with his familiar, pleasant tone. “Sometimes, what we worry about we bring about.”

“That’s a scary thought. But I think I understand. I vaguely remember saying the same thing to Tiny. Thank you, Cyrus.”

"You're welcome. Now would you like to join us for a midnight cruise?"

"I'll pass," she said, with a queasy smile. "As you know, heights are not one of my favorite pastimes. I'll just keep on rocking and enjoying the stars with my feet on something solid."

"Ah, the old rocking chair," chuckled Cyrus. "It relaxes the mind and exercises the body without much effort." With the tip of his wing, he gave Roberta a tender touch. Turning, he called out, "Okay, Tiny. If you're ready to go."

A gleeful voice from the adjacent room was loud and clear. "I'm ready. Let's go for it!"

And so they did, with Tiny riding high on a wing under a moonlit sky. "Wheee!" he shouted. "I've never had so much fun!"

When Tiny was ready, and not a moment sooner, Cyrus took Tiny for a variety of aerobatics and several upside down spins. "Hold on tight!" he bellowed. "Here comes another triple loop. Bottoms up!"

"Woo Hoo!" Tiny cried out again. "If my parents could see me now! I'm flying higher than an Eagle!"

With the light of a golden moon and a few shooting stars, Cyrus and Tiny flew back to the Sky Home. Later that night, Tiny was fast asleep, dreaming of his midnight flight with his zillions and zillions of bright, sparkling stars.

Chapter 26

"Is that a worried look I see on someone's pretty face?" asked Cyrus humorously. "Usually, rocking and frowning are unknown companions."

"Oh. Hi. How was your midnight cruise?"

"DE-LIGHT-FUL! Tiny's free spirit and your appreciation of Nature have added joy to my humble abode. Now my good friend, what about this look of worry. Do you want to share what's going on in that busy head of yours?"

Roberta slowly nodded as Cyrus took the antique rocking chair next to hers. "I must be a slow learner," she said with a heavy sigh. "I'm still thinking about that spotted Cat."

"You a slow learner?" chuckled Cyrus, rocking to and fro. "Now who's being modest?"

Roberta shrugged her shoulders. During their silent interval, the only sounds with the high winds were the creaking of two rocking chairs.

Since there was no reply, Cyrus continued. "It appears that you have the Cheetah by the tail and can't let go."

A distraught Roberta let loose a heavy sigh. "I feel so vulnerable. I know he's out to get me. It's just a matter of time."

"Then use your time wisely, Roberta."

"In other words, stop worrying," she sighed again. "That's easy for you to say."

Cyrus slowly nodded his head. "Worry and guilt are at the opposite ends of the same twig. Long ago, in my struggling youth, The Elder told me I could make my life easier by learning to fly in the space I occupy."

"Whoa! What do you mean by that?"

"It means to stay in the here and now. By doing so we eliminate wasted energy and allow life to be the joy it was intended to be. Then, as your Mom would say, move forward."

"In other words, give up worry before it destroys our moment of joy. Besides," she added with a flick of her ears, "that Cheetah might not even be at the Grand Assembly."

There followed a deliberate pause. Since Roberta didn't ask, Cyrus did not feel a need to comment on the appearance of the Cheetah. But knowing his reputation and popularity, the Cheetah would be there - - - and with his many friends.

"Cyrus, speaking of big Cats," she said with a sly grin, "do you know what happened to that outlawed Tiger? We had an *unfriendly* encounter, which he'll probably never forget."

"The Saber-toothed Tiger is no longer with us."

"Oh," she replied, not a bit surprised. "What happened to the old brute?"

"The Tiger decided he didn't want to die a slow, agonizing death by starvation. So he attacked a family of adult Lions. And to give credit to the Lions, who are ruled by a wise and fair-minded King, they made quick work of the Tiger so he wouldn't suffer needlessly."

"Well, as far as I'm concerned, that demon got what he deserved."

"Roberta, if you want to continue to grow," he said without malice, "you'll need to rise to a higher level of understanding. Everyone gets what they *create* and not what they *deserve.*"

Still rocking side-by-side, Roberta scratched her furry head, trying hard to put it all together. When she thought she understood, her reply was slow and deliberate. "Like when I worry about the Cheetah, I just make matters worse."

"And when you put yourself in a *hole,* or are feeling rejected, all you need to do is- - - "

"Ask for help," she interrupted. "And when I find myself in a hole, stop digging."

"That's correct," affirmed Cyrus. "I knew you were a fast study."

Roberta broke off a quick smile. Then after a considerable delay, she asked pensively, "Cyrus, what was the Saber's name?"

"Thomas. In his prime the other Meat Eaters called him Sir Thomas. In the eye of the Tiger, he was a great warrior. Then as he aged, he turned on his own kind."

"Why?" she asked thoughtfully.

"The whys are not important," grinned Cyrus. "Only the hows and the whooos."

"Are you joshing?"

"Not really. There could be a thousand whys and everyone a lie. Let's just say that Sir Thomas lost his way."

"And for his violent behavior, the Great Spirit punished him."

Cyrus, choosing his woods carefully, replied, "Actually, there are those who believe that we are not punished *for* our deeds, but *by* them. What goes around comes around." Cyrus paused for a moment then added, "There are many who believe that our Great Spirit Loves everyone unconditionally, including Sir Thomas."

Roberta again scratched her head. In deep thought, she decided to change the subject. "Cyrus, what do you mean by oneness?"

Following a moment of reflection, Cyrus appeared more solemn than usual. "Oneness is to never offend another Creature's body or mind. It means to be free of manipulation and unkind teasing. When someone says no it means just that. No doesn't mean yes or maybe or later. Oneness is being respectful of others and of their needs."

Roberta, her eyes unsteady was feeling somewhat uncomfortable, but not knowing why - - - exactly. Regaining her composure, which was taking a little longer than usual, she took her time to collect her thoughts, then said softly, "When you touch me, it's with the softness of the wings of a Butterfly. And when I want my oneness, you release me as soft as a Butterfly flutters from flower to flower."

There followed a quiet interlude as two figures remained silhouetted against the dark, blue sky. For the moment, the only sounds were the creaking vibrations of their wooden rocking chairs.

When Cyrus spoke his voice was as gentle as a whisper, as if not to disturb the serenity that was. "Roberta, your appreciation of Nature reflects your inner awareness."

Even though Roberta was feeling self-conscious, she remembered her decorum. "Thank you for those kind words, but Cyrus, how did you become so wise?"

"Roberta, by being a good listener. I've learned to listen to everyone and everything. The stars. A grain of sand. The wind. The - - -"

"The trees!" she interjected with growing interest.

"Yes, Roberta. Trees are excellent teachers. From the infinite sky to the eternal sea, from the smallest drop of rain to the highest mountain. All things are equally my teachers, including you and Tiny."

"Really? I always wanted to be a teacher. But I don't believe that Tiny knows anything about teaching."

"Have you not learned by being his friend?" inquired Cyrus with that gleam in his eye.

"Ummm," mused Roberta. "Yes, I guess I have. Patience for one. And I'm learning how to control my temper - - - er, sometimes," she added with a timid smile. "But how does he do it?"

"By example."

"Is that the best way to teach? By example?"

"Some say it's the *only* way to teach."

"Oh," replied Roberta, sounding a bit guarded. "Well, I really do want to be a good teacher. But I know now that teaching is more demanding than I ever imagined."

Cyrus nodded. "To be a teacher of merit, one needs to be a good student and a very good listener. That's essential."

From his rocking chair, Cyrus reached over and gently caressed Roberta with the tip of his wing. "Every experience," he continued, "brings us a learning opportunity. And for those who want to teach need to learn how to observe without judgment and to overcome the need to control others. Many years ago, The Elder shared that a wise teacher makes teaching and learning a joy."

Roberta was again feeling uneasy, but not knowing why - - - exactly. She thought it best to move on to another concern of hers. Strange, though, there was a feeling *deep down inside* resisting her need to ask. Pushing that resistance aside, and assuming that she knew what Cyrus would say, she proceeded. "Cyrus, what do you think of my Crusade?"

His reply was direct but kind. "Roberta, I may be wrong, but I have come to believe that there are no real crusades."

Nearly falling from her chair, Roberta stared motionless. It was as though she had been totally rejected. "What? What do you mean by that?"

"Roberta, what I believe to be important is how we feel about ourselves and the level of kindness we treat others, rather than the need to seek glory and fame."

After a very long delay, Roberta was still unsure of what to say. "I'm completely confused. I thought my Crusade was a great idea."

"Roberta, follow your heart, and be not concerned by what others may say about you or your endeavors. As for your confusion, it means you are in the process of learning."

"Well, I must be learning a whole bunch because I feel like I'm being buried by it."

Cyrus smiled to himself, charmed by Roberta's childlike openness. He knew that someday, when she would allow herself to see with her heart, she would understand.

"Cyrus, what if my proposal is defeated? What then?"

"One tree falls, a stronger growing by."

Roberta lowered her eyes. Again, trying hard to understand, a puzzled expression swept across her face.

Cyrus chose to give Roberta time to reflect, as he continued to rock with an easy rhythm all his own.

Roberta, again rocking to and fro, rubbed her furry chin. "If one idea fails, there will always be new opportunities."

"Nature's precocious child," he whispered. Then adding a new thought, Cyrus shared, "Life goes on in one form or another, be it a tree, or a distant star, or us."

"Well, I sincerely hope it's us!" blurted Roberta.

Amused, a lighthearted chuckle blended with the creaking rhythm of two old rocking chairs.

Moments later, Roberta hopped out of her chair and approached Cyrus, who opened up his powerful wings to receive her. After a quiet moment, she withdrew from his warm embrace. As before, she was released without resistance.

"Oneness," she quietly mused, "the wings of a Butterfly." Then returning to her rocker, she turned to Cyrus with an inquisitive look in her eye. "What do you plan to do with all your knowledge?"

On his hard beak a soft smile appeared. "There are times I would enjoy forgetting everything I have learned and just be who I am."

Speechless, Roberta stared at Cyrus, now more confused than ever.

The moon was completing its journey across the evening sky. Cyrus was now rocking alone listening to the sounds of the night. Nearby, Roberta had fallen asleep, dreaming of her Great Crusade.

Chapter 27

Roberta had deliberately set her mind to wake up before dawn. If she had her way, she was not about to miss an opportunity to see her morning star.

With a new day dawning, Roberta raced up the stairs to the east balcony. Both balconies were about three steps above the circular ceiling. This made it possible to see in every direction, with the only obstruction being the cone-shaped pinnacle that extended up and between the twin balconies.

As Roberta looked about, she was enveloped by the pre-dawn gray. Standing alone, she made a complete turn to capture the panoramic view. Now, facing the empty horizon, she waited with growing anticipation for her first sunrise.

Moments slowly passed by. Then with the upper tip of the red, fiery ball, the distant skyline was broken. "Here comes the sun," she sighed. "My morning star." Her opened arms were fully extended, ready to receive the warmth of the early morning sun.

Overhead, as the sun made its way up and over the rim, the gray sky gave way to a blend of radiant yellows and reds. "It's beautiful," she sighed again. "You were a treat worth waiting for. Who could have guessed that I would see my first sunrise with a mile high view? As Cyrus said, all things happen at the perfect time."

Within the stillness, Roberta listened to the sounds of the awakening world. She closed her eyes and thought she heard her name being carried by the wind. She stood absolutely still. This time there was no doubt.

"Ro- -ber- -ta! Ro- -ber- -ta!"

But it wasn't the wind. It was the cheerful voice of Tiny. "Come on Ro- -ber- -ta. Breakfast is red- -deee!"

Mildly upset that her private interlude was interrupted, she took a deep breath. "Everything, even breakfast, has its perfect time," she said, thinking of what she had learned with Cyrus. "Besides, life is too marvelous to waste it on anger." She then allowed herself a serene moment before calling back. "Tiii- -neee. I'm commm - - - minggg!"

During breakfast, Tiny was heard to say, "Cyrus is it all right to change my mind? I would like to have some blueberries."

"Tiny," Cyrus responded affectionately, "you may change your mind as often as the wind changes its direction. Allow me to fetch the few that we have left."

"Thank you, Cyrus. Blueberries will *always* be my favorite dessert."

After breakfast and the chores completed, it was time to return to what Cyrus fondly called Mother Earth. Roberta asked if there was time for one more glimpse of the mile-high view. There was and Cyrus gave a consenting nod.

As for Tiny, flying was his delight. This time he knew what to expect, and it increased his excitement even more. "I'm ready to fly," he cheered.

Cyrus reached over and gave him a gentle touch. "Yes, Tiny. I do believe you are. Your enthusiasm shall always be a reminder for me to stay forever young."

Tiny beamed. "I like compliments."

When Roberta made her return, Cyrus' vibrant voice was heard: "Hold on Tiny! Hold on Roberta! We're off!"

Down- - - Down- - - Down - - -

"Wheee!" Tiny shouted, "I love flying! I'm ready to turn in my shell for a pair of wings!"

"Don't be silly," grinned Roberta. "You can't do that."

Undaunted by her rejection, Tiny responded, "Maybe next time. Huh, Cyrus?"

"Yes, Tiny. As the Caterpillar becomes the Butterfly, you, too, shall have your own wings to fly."

"Woo Hoo!" Tiny sang out as loud as he could. "Woo Hoo!"

Roberta, thinking she had said something wrong, became subdued. When she heard Cyrus call her name, her fear that he was disappointed was swept away by the kindness of his voice.

She turned and was greeted by a big smile. "For a young lady that used to get dizzy whenever higher than a hole in the ground, you have come a long way. May your continued growth inspire me to a higher awareness."

Roberta, not expecting to hear such praise, felt overwhelmed. Following a moment of indecision, she returned his smile and said, "Thank you, Cyrus."

"Wheee!" Tiny shouted again. "Flying is for me!"

"Hold on!" bellowed Cyrus. "We're approaching Mother Earth!"

Chapter 28

With his wings slightly arched, Cyrus glided to a smooth landing. Well, except for one unexpected bump, which prompted him to cry out, "Whoops!" Then, turning his head towards Roberta, he flashed a playful grin, "Excuse me."

Back on Mother Earth, they joined together under the grand tree, with Tiny and Roberta playfully competing for Cyrus' attention. Each tugged from a wing as they twirled him 'round-and-'round-and-' round.

Roberta was the first to let go, giving Tiny the opening to take both wings of their willing partner. Around the tree they whirled, skipping and jumping to and fro, while Roberta, dancing free, took her turn to watch.

When Tiny and Cyrus twirled on by for a third time, Roberta saw an open wing. Spontaneously, she reached out and felt the firm hold of his feathery grip. With a squeak, hoot, and a holler, the threesome held on together as they danced and skipped about.

Tiny, still holding on tight, raised his hind legs off the ground, calling out, "Look! I'm flying again!"

Cyrus hooted and whistled with delight, while Roberta's long ears were thumping with joy.

Then, together they all fell to the ground in one big heap, laughing and hooting as they did.

Catching their breath beneath the tree's shady branches, Cyrus laughed out loud, "I surrender! I surrender! You got me good." His two young playmates eased up, and Cyrus lowered his wings, giving each of them a tender squeeze. "Never have I received so much for doing what I enjoy doing most. I thank you both dearly for sharing this time with an old Bird like me. The time we have shared together, I'll long remember with fond memories. And- - -"

"Me, too!" interrupted Roberta.

"Me, three!" followed Tiny, creating a new round of laughter.

When Tiny and Roberta had settled down a bit, Cyrus took that opportunity to complete what he had started to share. "Before we say farewell, I want to express my gratitude for all the joy you two have brought into my life. For that and more, you have my eternal friendship."

"And thank you, Cyrus, for everything you have done for Tiny and me. You are everything they say about you."

"And more!" chimed in Tiny, and for the moment, forgetting all about his need to be shy. "I've had so much fun: Flying across the sky, the neat head tricks, the squeaky rocking chairs, the blueberries, sleeping all night in a circular bed, and - - - and - - -"

Tiny was so excited that he just couldn't keep up with his own enthusiasm. Trying to catch his runaway thoughts, Cyrus was quicker. "Tiny, you continue to amaze me with your pure energy."

With a childlike smile, Tiny had something he wanted to say. "This may be pretty hard for a little Turtle to do, but I'm going to give you a BIG BEAR HU G." And he did. And a misty-eyed Cyrus enjoyed it completely.

Roberta, forgetting her own thoughts for the moment, soon joined in, cottontail and all. When Tiny and Roberta looked up, they could see the love that was there in his eyes.

Cyrus, letting go a heavy sigh, placed his powerful wings gently around their shoulders. "My dear ones, it is time for us to part for awhile. When we meet at the Grand Assembly, we can share our joy anew."

"I'll bring mine!" cheered Tiny.

"I can hardly believe this has all happened," said Roberta with an obvious tremor in her voice. "Your acceptance of Tiny and me; your support for my Crusade; and knowing that the three of us will be together again working for a peaceful kingdom. It's - - - it's so wonderful, I could cry."

"Remember, it's okay to cry," offered Tiny.

"Today's tears of joy," expressed Cyrus, "will caress the sorrows of yesterday and the ones yet unseen."

Roberta brushed away a tear and looked at Cyrus with that mock frown of hers, slowly shaking her head.

Cyrus chuckled. "You're right, my dear. I should leave the poetry to others."

"I like your poetry," ventured Tiny with his green eyes doing their dance.

"Thank you, Tiny," he said with a big wink. "I needed that."

For the moment, Roberta's playfulness had run its course. With her usual, serious demeanor, she remembered what she wanted to ask, even though she was certain she already knew the answer. "Cyrus, I have a very important question for you."

"All right my dear. I'm all ears," causing Tiny to laugh.

"Hey! That's my line," blurted Roberta, pretending to be miffed. Then turning to Tiny. "And why are you laughing? You didn't think it was funny when I said it."

Tilting his head to one side, Tiny grinned, "I've learned something since then." Then playfully he said, "What were you going to ask Cyrus? I'm all ears."

Roberta put her right paw on her hip and gave Tiny a long look. "Tiny, I do believe you like playing with my mind."

With that look of innocence, Tiny hooted, "Whooo me?"

Cyrus, smiling to himself, quietly observed them play out their little charade.

Roberta slowly shook her furry head, then shifted her full attention back to Cyrus. With increasing anticipation she said, "Cyrus, you will be the one to present my proposal to the Grand Assembly. Won't you?"

The question caught Tiny by surprise, but Cyrus replied without any hesitation. "The answer to your question is no. The one chosen to be the keynote speaker is someone wiser and more deserving than I."

Roberta's long ears became lifeless, drooping down the sides of her pale cheeks. She was devastated.

Tiny blinked, his pointed tail now hanging limp.

What they had heard just couldn't be true. In their eyes, Cyrus was the wisest, most caring Creature who had ever lived. No one could possibly be more deserving than their Cyrus.

During their strained silence, a coy grin appeared on Tiny's face. "You're joshing us. Right?"

"No Tiny. I wouldn't mislead you and Roberta on something as important as the Grand Assembly."

Roberta was still visibly crushed. "But if not you, Cyrus, who will be the main speaker?"

"The chosen one is called The Elder. To receive this high honor, one must have acquired wisdom, compassion, and spiritual insights. With these qualities, The Elder excels all others."

"Then, who is The Elder?" asked Roberta, her voice a mixture of disappointment and curiosity.

"Your question is a fair one, but I have a sworn commitment not to reveal the identity of The Elder." Then sounding less mysterious, he stated, "But I am at liberty to say that at the Grand Assembly, I have the privilege of introducing The Elder, my friend and mentor."

It was obvious by the looks on their faces, especially Roberta's, that they were still deeply disappointed. Cyrus offered a few more words of reassurance before allowing them to choose how they would handle their own feelings.

Roberta, very much unlike herself, stood there speechless. Tiny decided to take advantage of Roberta's despondence. With a tilt of his head, he playfully teased, "Could you give us a little hint whooo the speaker will be?"

Again, Roberta was quick to judge that Tiny was being disrespectful, and was about to tell him so, when Cyrus replied spontaneously, "Tiny, I accept your request as a challenge to my creativity, such as it is."

Tiny let loose a big grin, while Roberta's face revealed her embarrassment. She was relieved when nothing was said about her behavior.

Cyrus immediately commenced his performance. With one wing, he pointed towards the sky, while the other wing supported his feathered chin. He appeared both deep in thought and playful at the same time. His efforts were not wasted on Tiny, who didn't even try to smoother his giggles.

"Hmmm. Maybe you can find a clue or two in this simple riddle."

While Tiny was just happy watching Cyrus put on his goofy display, Roberta was determined to solve the riddle.

Cyrus, exaggerating his every move, began the challenge:

"Without the power of this creative
Critter, there would be
No Birds to sing
No flowers in spring
No life to be
Not you or me."

Two curious faces stared at each other, then quickly back to Cyrus. They were completely dumfounded, but only one of them truly cared.

Choosing to ignore their bewilderment, and not wanting to give Roberta time to respond to his poetic endeavor, Cyrus offered them a new experience. "Before we say farewell, I would like to form a circle."

Instantly, Tiny knew this was something he wanted to do and was the first to follow Cyrus' lead.

Roberta, trying hard to solve the riddle, declined his invitation.

Cyrus hesitated, and for a brief moment there seemed to be a look of disappointment. Following a deep sigh, he proceeded to do what he had intended to do, but with only a partner of one.

Roberta stood alone and watched Cyrus and Tiny form their circle. At that moment, for some unexplained reason, she decided to join them. When she made her approach, Cyrus and Tiny, without saying a word, opened up to include her.

Moments passed by, as they continued to stand in their motionless circle. Then, without any apparent effort of their own, their circle of three seemed to create its own special and mystical force. United as one, they would rock backwards on their heels, then weaved forward on their toes. It was unlike anything Roberta and Tiny had ever before experienced.

Together, as they weaved and rocked, the soft, soothing voice of Cyrus seemed to extent their rapture. "As with life, our circle has no beginning or ending. But our circle does have a center. And we are all It!" At that very moment, Cyrus gave them both an affectionate squeeze.

Some time much later, Roberta will remember repeating after Cyrus, "Thank you so much."

Under the multicolored leaves, their circle continued to sway in and out, and side to side. Beyond time, all was serene as they shared their enchanted moment together. Their long silence was broken when Tiny said, "Cyrus, I need a big hug."

"One of my bear hugs?" assumed Cyrus, preparing to do just that. But he stopped short when he heard Tiny respond with a playful NO. There was a mischievous look on his face.

"What?" said Cyrus with a quizzical grin, while Roberta stood by wondering what was going on.

Tiny's grin reached all the way to his pointed ears. "This time I want a BIG OWL HUG!"

"I do believe," thought Roberta amused, "that the little Turtle has done it to the big Bird."

Whether true or not, Cyrus reached down and swept Tiny off his feet, giving him the biggest hug he had ever received.

Roberta stepped aside, satisfied just to watch the two of them embrace. Cyrus offered no objection or encouragement, allowing Roberta to be Roberta. And to have her oneness.

Chapter 29

Cyrus stood alone before pushing off with his sturdy legs. Extending his five-foot wing span, he made his way skyward. Suspended high overhead with the wind, he watched the two young compadres cross the circular clearing. When Tiny and Roberta reached the giant-sized trees, they turned to wave their last goodbye. Cyrus tipped his wing and called out, "May your journey home be safe and joyful. My dear friends, farewell."

Still waving, Roberta and Tiny turned and disappeared into the Dark Forest.

Making their way through the trees, Roberta was still feeling the euphoria she had experienced while in their circle with Cyrus. Naturally she wanted to share her experience with Tiny.

"Tiny, while in our circle, I experienced sensations I never knew I had. There were moments I was overwhelmed with deep feelings of peace and joy, all in one. I could feel shivers moving up my back. It was pure energy."

Roberta took a deep breath, her eyes aglow with wonder. "Then something really strange began to happen to me. Tiny, even with all those marvelous feelings, there were moments I was overcome with fear. It was as though I was drifting off to somewhere unreal. Or nowhere - - - with no way to get back! And believe me, that's scary."

"I know that feeling for sure," Tiny said, his face expressing a look of keen interest.

After going a short distance, Roberta asked Tiny had he experienced anything special while in their circle with Cyrus.

Tiny took his time, trying to recapture that moment. "Ummm," he finally replied, slow and easy. "I can remember feeling special only when his feathers slipped inside my shell. It tickled," he said with a flow of giggles.

Roberta flicked her long ears, feeling a tinge of irritation. "Can't he ever be serious?" she thought. Before allowing her displeasure to get the best of her, she wondered what Cyrus would say. Following a long delay, she reached over and gave Tiny a gentle touch. "Tiny, I guess I needed that."

Step by step, they continued on, neither one saying a word. Similar to their first journey, the monstrous-sized trees blocked out the morning sun. They were now surrounded by dark, gloomy shadows.

Then, to Roberta's surprise, Tiny left her side and was about to disappear among the trees. "Tiny, where are you going?"

"I'll be right back," he replied, as he vanished into the darkness.

Concerned about Tiny's welfare, Roberta stopped and waited for his return. Her first thought was that he was searching for something to eat. But then she couldn't help but wonder if Tiny might be possessed by some lingering thoughts of the curse. She was just about to call out his name when he reappeared.

"You're right," said Tiny cheerfully.

Robert scratched her furry head. It was reassuring to see that Tiny was all right, but she was also a little mystified. After a moment of hesitation, she asked, "Right about what, Tiny?"

"These trees are marvelous."

Roberta blinked, thinking that maybe she had misunderstood. But more surprises were soon to follow.

"And Roberta, there is no curse. It's all in the head, just like you said."

She was feeling a sense of self-satisfaction, but before Rapid Roberta could respond, Tiny reached up to give her a fistful of golden- colored flowers.

"For me?" she gulped.

Tiny nodded as Roberta accepted her gift.

"Thank you, Tiny. Thank you very much." At that very moment Roberta felt closer to Tiny then ever before.

Tiny looked up into her misty eyes. "Remember Roberta's law. It's okay to cry."

"Yes I know," she said softly. "I was also thinking of the time when you told me that the only good flower was one you could eat. And now - - -" She stopped, unable to find the words to express her feelings.

Tiny looked up to Roberta and said, "I remember saying that. But I've learned something since then. I *have* a good teacher."

Roberta placed her soft, furry paw around his shoulder. "Tiny, I do believe you have outgrown your teacher. I think it's time for me to retire."

Together, homeward bound, they made their way through the Dark Forest, enjoying the wonders that surrounded them. And the feelings they had discovered *deep down inside.*

Chapter 30

At last - - - the eve of the Grand Assembly. An anxious Roberta had returned to her favorite meadow. There she watched the luminous sun dip beyond the skyline. The day surrendered to twilight, then to darkness.

For Roberta it was the longest six days of her life. But tomorrow could be the beginning of a new world, or just one more day that the opportunity to make a difference would slip away like so many times before.

But there was no doubt that the Grand Assembly was on everyone's mind. There was no one alive that could remember anything that caused so much commotion or controversy. The entire kingdom and a young Roberta vibrated with excitement.

Now, nestled in her cozy bed, the anticipation of the grand affair was just too much for her, and falling asleep was a thousand thoughts away.

Naturally her Mom and Pop, and her grandparents, were bubbling with pride. They knew their first born would amount to something very special. "Why it was in her blood," they would all proudly say.

Roberta's sisters and brothers were too young to truly appreciate what Roberta had accomplished. The Bunnies, however, were definitely aware of one thing: They found Roberta a little strange since her time away from home. It was as though she wasn't the same big sister they had grown up with. For one thing, she was more preoccupied with her thoughts. She was also less bossy. That they liked.

During Roberta's absence, there were other changes, too. She now had nine sisters and nine brothers. Surprise! Surprise!

Still unable to sleep, Roberta's mind continued jumping from one thought to another. She recalled how curiosity had gotten the best of her. Like with so many others, she had tried to discover the identity of The Elder. While doing so, she met a number of those who were fervently opposed to the whole concept of the Grand Assembly. Some were against Roberta's proposal just because they were fearful of the very idea of change. For them, it was better to live with what they had, Meat Eaters and all, then to risk the unknown.

The most vehement protests came from the hated and despised Queen Cobra. She argued bitterly that any scheme to change what she considered the natural order of things, to be dangerous, unworkable, and totally unrealistic.

Queen Cobra and her followers were not to be taken lightly. They were quick to strike, spreading their poisonous ideas against the Grand Assembly. They even went so far as to accuse The Elder and Cyrus as being leaders of a conspiracy to take over the kingdom.

In spite of the Mean Queen's deadly influence, there was a rumor that a small band of Cobras were in open rebellion against her coldhearted tyranny.

But as promising as that might sound, it was negated by the disturbing reality that the Lions, the most powerful of all the Meat Eaters, were completely loyal to their king. It was understood that King Lion ruled his pride with absolute authority. But the King was also known for his wisdom and integrity. As Cyrus had stated, King Lion was fair-minded. Evidently, the Saber-toothed Tiger knew it, too.

Over the last few days, Roberta also met a very large group who were as supportive of the Grand Assembly as King Lion and Queen Cobra were opposed. This pack of Pachyderms, by and large, favored all humane causes. With the solid leadership of Edi and Eddy Elephant, they trumpeted their steadfast support for a peaceful kingdom.

Roberta met another group who was completely indifferent to the Grand Assembly, and everything else for that matter. This group didn't actually have a leader, but by default, Osbert Ostrich was left in command, such as it was. His group wasn't for or against Roberta's proposal. Non-involvement was their motto. In his own dubious words, Osbert stated,

"We're irreversibly indifferent to the success or failure of the Grand Assembly, now and forever."

Some wondered if Osbert would ever get his head out of the sand long enough to make one important commitment in his life. When asked, he replied, as he was putting his head back into the sand, that he didn't care to take a stand one way or the other. Of course, it was difficult to talk this way, and his muffled words were not always understood.

But there was one thing for certain. Everyone planned to be present at the biggest, most exciting event in almost three hundred years. Many were going just to see The Elder. There was some speculation that The Elder was a Turtle or an Elephant because they have such a long life and have excellent memories. A stronger claim was made for Glenn Giraffe. He was not only very wise, but his compassion for the weak and defenseless was legendary. And because of his spiritual qualities, he was head and shoulders above all the others.

Roberta, tossing and turning, was still wide awake. Disturbing thoughts of the vengeful Cat persisted. Trying to follow Cyrus' suggestion, and not to worry, she asked the Great Spirit to put the Cheetah in his proper place. "That should do quite nicely," she whispered.

.And even though Roberta had tried extra hard to break Cyrus' riddle, all her efforts failed. "Well, maybe next time," she thought to herself.

Roberta turned over again, still struggling to fall asleep. And even though she was restless, there was now a soft smile on her face. "Tomorrow I'll see Tiny, my good friend. And at high noon, The Elder's identity will be revealed. He really must be someone special to be the keynote speaker. And Cyrus. I can hardly wait to see him again. It's been a long six days without him. But each passing moment brings me closer to Cyrus. And my Great Crusade."

Was there any wonder why Roberta was so enraptured? These thoughts danced through her head right up to the moment that slumber had its way.

Chapter 31

A stout figure was standing alone on an open balcony. Silhouetted against the early morning gray, Cyrus took a long look at the rising sun. "Everyday is beautiful," he said softly. "And some days are more beautiful than others." Turning to the west, he prayed: "Great Spirit, if it be your will, may this be the day our kingdom returns to the paradise we lost so long ago. And with your blessings, may my journey be safe and the arrival of everyone be at the perfect time."

Cyrus extended his powerful wings. With a downward flap, he lifted off into the silver-gray sky. In flight, even though he was challenged by a strong headwind, he flew with an easy, steady motion.

Flying westward, his thoughts were miles away. "I never knew seven sunrises could pass by so slowly. It will do my heart good to see Tiny and Roberta again."

For no apparent reason, Roberta awoke from a short, but sound sleep. Quickly, she hopped out of bed and scampered down the tunnel of her underground home. With the sleep still in her eyes, she popped her head out of her hole. She blinked from the early, hazy light. Her morning star was already beyond the horizon, just missing her second sunrise.

Then, "Cyrus" she whispered. "Are you on your way?" A strange, wonderful feeling came over her.

Chapter 32

Roberta was too excited to have breakfast. And since she also wanted to be the first one to arrive for the Grand Assembly, she decided to skip the purple cabbage and orange juice.

Mom knew by the look in her baby's eyes, that Roberta could not be persuaded to take time to have a good breakfast. However, when Roberta thought she could save time by dispensing with goodbye hugs, her Mom had the last word.

Their hugs were followed by Mom's tender words, while Pop stood proudly by. Roberta was anxious to leave, but it was too late. Her sisters and brothers were now awake, and they, too, wanted their hugs - - - all eighteen of them.

Roberta began to fuss even though she knew that when her Mom made up her mind, there was no sense to argue. So she didn't. Well, not too much.

Her eighteen siblings stood in a large circle. Starting with the oldest, each in turn received a hug from their big sister, albeit, a quick one.

Roberta was now all set to go. With her famous jack-rabbit start, she zoomed off waving a hurried goodbye. "See you at the Grand Assembly!" she called back. With a quick turn of her head, she was soon out of sight.

Mom and Pop continued to gaze down the path long after their Roberta had disappeared from view. Together, arm in arm, they would worry and wonder about their first born.

Somewhat behind schedule, and still determined to be the first to arrive at the park, Rapid Roberta turned up her speed. With a smile and a wave, she streaked passed those who had gotten off to an early start. They were soon left far behind.

With her speed, it was easy for Roberta to make up for lost time, and there over the next rise, her destination appeared in the distance. With extra effort, she increased her speed, and quicker than a Bee can sting, she was where she wanted to be.

Screeching to a halt, she glanced about. Immediately, Roberta was astonished by the park's natural beauty. "Without a doubt this site is a marvelous sight. And visa versa," she added with a grin.

But her joy was short lived. No, it wasn't the over-spotted Cheetah. But there in the clearing, she saw a flock of Flamingos mingling in a sparkling pond. Some of the "Early Birds," as they would someday be known, had arrived before dawn.

With a shrug, Roberta said to herself, "Win some, lose some." Pushing away her disappointment, she decided to enjoy her surroundings. There was no need to hurry, so she didn't. She had plenty of time. Eventually, she hoped to find Tiny and Cyrus, and the sooner the better.

"What a gorgeous garden," she sighed. The tall, lush evergreens appeared to blend with the high, blue sky. She breathed in deeply. The scent of brightly colored flowers of reds, yellows, greens, blacks, blues, and orange filled the air with a refreshing fragrance.

Slowly turning around, not wanting to miss anything, her eyes gazed over the landscape. Roberta couldn't imagine a more beautiful spot in the entire Jungle Kingdom. For her, this garden was the perfect place for the Grand Assembly.

While Roberta was preoccupied with her tour of the park, Creatures of every color and scent were arriving. One enormous Elephant, with his extended trunk, trumpeted a morning serenade. The blast was so loud, she wondered if it might wake the dead. "But they're not invited," chuckled Roberta.

When some of the Elephants recognized Roberta, they gave her an enthusiastic greeting, waving their leathery trunks. With a spontaneous smile, she waved back and thanked them for their support.

Moving deeper into the park, she was greeted by those who supported her cause. There were waves and high hopes for everyone. She was feeling marvelous.

Then, Roberta shuddered all the way to her pink toes. There, crossing her path was Cyn-thia Cobra who hissed her contempt. As the Cobra slithered down the winding path, still hissing with her thin, slippery tongue, Roberta was no longer feeling overconfident. "I guess I needed that. Huh, Cyrus?"

Trying to regain her composure, which was taking a little longer than usual, thoughts of Cyn-thia continued. "Those cold-blooded Vipers really do get to me," shuddered Roberta. I wonder if I'll ever be able to see a slippery Snake without quivering."

Even so, she thought it was better to encounter a thousand poisonous Cobras than one vengeful Cheetah.

Still unnerved, she tried to concentrate on something more pleasant. "I got to find Tiny. I wonder where he is. Unless he gives himself plenty of time, he'll miss The Elder's presentation. And that would be terrible."

She also wondered where Cyrus could be. Although it was still quite early, she had the unpleasant feeling that her two friends would both arrive late, or not at all.

Coming to a bend in her path, a familiar face emerged from a small group. Edi Elephant excused herself and lumbered over to greet Roberta. After they exchanged praises and gratitude, they joined her small circle of friends.

Following the introductions, Roberta thanked them for their unyielding support, and they in turn, expressed that it was they who needed to be thanking her.

Roberta, feeling self-conscious, was much relieved when Pauline Black Panther offered to explain why she, a Meat Eater, was supporting Roberta's proposal. "I'm doing this for my young, for we have no defense against the increasing numbers of our greatest rivals, the Lions. The way I see it, our only chance of survival is to return to the time of non-violence."

Foxy Fran agreed totally. "Our numbers are decreasing rapidly. Something unique and daring must be done or we will be extinct within three generations."

Pierre Peacock fanned his brilliant, multicolored tail and said, "Foxy is much too modest to take the credit. But because of her art of diplomacy, she has convinced every adult Fox and a growing number of Cobras to vote for a peaceful kingdom."

"Hear! Hear!" cheered the circle of seven. "Hear! Hear!"

Foxy, with her clever eye, was quick to ask, "Are you all right, Roberta?"

"Oh? Er, yes. I'm okay," surprised that anyone would have noticed. "I have a thing with Snakes that makes me shudder. It's something I haven't yet learned to control. But I'm trying."

"There are many who have contempt for those poisonous Vipers," stated Bobby Bison.

"I know I do," conceded Goldie Gopher. "My home and loved ones have been attacked by Cobras more times than I care to remember."

"I know you speak the truth," Edi consoled. But if we hope to create a paradise for everyone, it's essential that we overcome our preconceived attitudes. There is no room for prejudice or hatred."

"Old hatreds die hard," offered Foxy. "But they do if you allow your heart to be filled with love and forgiveness."

"My family and I are working on it," said Goldie.

Bobby displayed his agreement by nodding his large head.

Pauline swished her Black tail and said proudly, "I've made contact with several of the rebelling Cobras, and they want the same things we want: A peaceful kingdom, free of hate and violence."

"Hear! Hear!" came their encircled call. "Hear! Hear!"

"We should never be afraid to change," said Goldie. "Any more than a Gopher should be afraid of darkness. And when a new challenge is accepted, always look for the light at the end of the tunnel."

"Foxy and I have done that," purred Pauline Panther. "And for our efforts, we have received both praise and condemnation. But our numbers are growing, and we're not turning back. We're willing to risk everything for the cause."

"Hear! Hear!" they surged. "Hear! Hear!"

"You and Foxy should be commended," expressed Goldie. "But we need to remember there are those who are as sincere in their beliefs as we are in ours. Therefore, as you talk with others, try to keep an open mind."

Roberta flicked her long ears. "I would like to respond to Goldie's statement. May I?"

"You certainly may," replied Edi, giving Roberta a caress with her trunk. "We're all family here."

Roberta now looking directly at Goldie, asserted, "I've put too much into this cause not to have strong feelings. To have an open mind concerning the value of creating a peaceful kingdom is like having no mind at all. To establish peace and justice for everyone, there can be no compromise! Either we go forward together or we will perish under the increasing threat of the Meat Eaters!"

"Hear! Hear!" their circle responded. "Hear! Hear!"

"To move forward is our commitment," confirmed Edi. Then with her vibrant voice, she declared, "A new age is upon us if we have the courage and wisdom to accept it. Within the laws of decency, we will do whatever it takes to be victorious."

Another series of cheers followed, as Roberta's appreciation for Edi was enhanced.

"Thank you, Roberta for speaking out," said Goldie. "I understand what you are saying and I will reconsider my point of view."

"Roberta, you have our complete loyalty to the very end," expressed Foxy. "And everyone here knows there are no guarantees."

"And we are willing to risk our lives," pledged Pierre Peacock.

"Hear! Hear!" made the rounds. "Hear! Hear!"

"Well, as for me," charged in Bobby, "I'll do whatever I can for Roberta's proposal. Not to, would condone the status quo of killing and destruction. I've heard from the herd, that we Bison stand united, for we are determined not to be helpless victims of some hungry, feline Beast. What can be gained by doing nothing when the issue is self-destruction or survival?"

Again a round of cheers was heard.

Pauline Black Panther swished her long tail. "What you say Roberta and Bobby makes sense. That's why we're here. To share ideas and learn."

"I'm ashamed to say that some of my friends are afraid of new ideas," revealed Goldie. "They fear that any change will eventually be controlled by the Meat Eaters."

"Will worry or fear change the future?" Not waiting for a reply, Foxy continued, her eyes taking everyone in. "I think not. It would serve us better to put our energies in trying to convince our opposition to see the merits of Roberta's proposal. And whatever you do, do it in such a manner that has the best chance in furthering our cause. And Goldie, there's no reason why you need to feel ashamed. There is none of us so perfect that we can't stand some improvement."

"I can see why they call you Foxy," smiled Goldie.

Proud Pierre fanned his iridescent tail. "Unlike some of my friends, Goldie, I'm an optimist, always praying for the best."

"That is wise," asserted Bobby. "It doesn't take any more energy to be an optimist, and it's far more rewarding."

"Exactly!" Pierre proclaimed. "Besides misery and heartbreak, what can be gained by being a pessimist? You, my extended family have taught me how to perceive the positive and bless the negative."

"Speaking of family," interjected Edi, "has anyone seen our friend, Glenn Giraffe?"

"I have," answered Bobby, bobbing his head. "Early this morning he was with a flock of Doves."

"Always with the defenseless," stated Pauline.

"Glenn's compassion and spiritual qualities are unequaled," Edi affirmed.

"I imagine that with his head high above the clouds, he would be inclined to be a spiritual being."

Light laughter encircled their group.

Edi smiled warmly. "Well said, Roberta. It's good for the heart to have a sense of humor, especially in times like these. Laughter helps to cut through the tension."

"Thank you, Edi. I've been told more than once that I take life too seriously. That I need to laugh more."

"Laughter is good for the soul," Pauline agreed softly.

Ideas and suggestions continued to make the rounds, while Roberta slipped into a deep silence. At the moment, other matters were dominating her thoughts. Foxy, with her clever eye, glanced over to Roberta, but this time she chose to keep her observations to herself.

When a stillness embodied their circle, Roberta took that opportunity to thank them again for their loyal support and friendship. "I must be on my way. I would like to find Tiny and Cyrus as soon as possible. I have a tendency to worry when things are out of my control."

"We understand, Roberta," assured Edi. "We can only imagine what this day must mean to you. Why, my dear child, you must have a thousand thoughts rushing through your head."

"Speaking on behave of all of those who believe in your cause," concluded Foxy, "whether your proposal wins the day or not, you and Tiny and Cyrus have our lifelong gratitude."

"Hear! Hear!" rallied the circle. "Hear! Hear!"

"Thank you, Foxy." Then turning to face each of her new friends, Roberta again expressed her gratitude. "Your commitment to our worthy cause means everything to me. Thank you one and all. And without Tiny and Cyrus, today's opportunity would still just a distant dream."

Before saying more, Roberta paused for a long moment. With her new friends, she felt a deep need to share a part of her painful past. With a measure of difficulty, Roberta began with a sadness in her voice: "When I was first born, a slither of Cobras took away my grandparents - - - and I still miss them dearly. For me, forgiveness comes hard."

A quiet moment embraced their circle. Pauline Panther, with empathy in her eyes, reached over and gave Roberta a tender touch.

"We're all sorry for your loss," consoled Edi. "Our deepest condolences for you and your family. It's never easy to accept the loss of a loved one. And as we all know, forgiveness is the only way to heal the heart."

"Yes I know," Roberta replied softly.

"Everyone in our kingdom has lost someone due to violence," shared Foxy, "that is why we are here today, to help regain our lost paradise."

A composed, "Hear! Hear!" was given.

With her leathery trunk, Edi gave Roberta another caress, then asked for a moment of quiet prayer. Someone suggested that Roberta take the center of their circle, but she quickly declined, saying that they were all equally involved.

Both Edi and Foxy concurred. Then, following Edi's lead, they bowed their heads.

In the heart of the Jungle, a small circle of uncommon friends united together in their quest for the common good.

Chapter 33

After a round of farewells, Roberta was on her way to look for Tiny and Cyrus. And she did, high and low, but with the same results. Then to her surprise, she heard someone calling her name. The unfamiliar voice sounded non-threatening but sibilant, causing cold shivers to go down her back. Roberta spun around, staring into the clear, black eyes of one of those cold-blooded Cobras. She could feel her whole body shake. With sheer determination, Roberta regained her composure. Well, almost.

"Allow me to introduce myself," hissed the Cobra, his wet, slippery tongue darting in and out of his skin-tight mouth. "My name isss CeZar. Are you Roberta, the one responsible for today's pro-cee-dings?"

Roberta did not enjoy being hissed at, but she promised Edi that she would try to overcome her ill-feelings she harbored against Snakes. But before she could say a word, her ears began to twitch. "Yes, I'm Roberta," she replied with a touch of civility. "And why do you ask?"

"I don't blame you for being susss-pish-shusss," lisped CeZar politely. "I can only quessss that thisss day must be very bisss-seee for you."

Even with his hissing, Robert was surprised by his decorum. "I have time." Then with some difficulty, she said, "Is there something I can do for you?"

"Actually, it'sss what I can do for you and your cause. There's been a small but sau-cesss-ful rebellion against Queen Cobra. And we want you to know that we will do all we can to make your proposal a sau-cesss."

For a moment, all that Roberta could do was shake her head in disbelief. "Why, that's marvelous. Thank you, CeZar. Our cause does need your support."

Roberta paused to look up, and realized that her ears had stopped their twitching. Well, almost. "I want to apologize for my behavior if I was offensive in any way."

"Not at all," smiled CeZar. "I'm much aware of the hatred that we Cobrasss must bear every day. It a-peersss that rumors survive where truth isss ignored. But that'sss another story. I'll be going now. And may our Great SSSpirit be with you."

As Roberta watched CeZar disappear down the narrow path, she stood there thinking how far events have gone all because Tiny and she went searching for Cyrus the Great.

Roberta's thoughts were interrupted when she heard a rumor that Tiny had been seen down by the river with a family of Reptiles. Her anticipation of seeing Tiny was real, but then, it was only a rumor.

Then, too, no one had seen Cyrus. Those who knew him were reassuring, saying that he would appear on time. They insisted that not even a persistent headwind would keep Cyrus from performing his responsibilities. They reminded Roberta that the keynote address was scheduled for high noon, which still left plenty of time. So there was no need for her to worry.

Willing, but unable to follow their sound advice, Roberta went on with her anxious search. Also, thoughts of that vengeful Cheetah continued to be heavy on her mind. Moving quickly with a turn to the right and down the lane, Roberta came to an abrupt stop. Her long ears began to thump. "Hey! Where have you been? I've been worried, er, I mean I've been looking all over for you."

"Oh, I've been with some of my new friends," Tiny said cheerfully.

Putting her paw on her hip, and pretending to be mildly upset, she said, "You've been entertaining yourself, while I've been all over this place searching for you, thinking that maybe you were lost or something far worse."

"Yep. And you don't need to worry about me."

"Who said I was worried?"

"You did," countered Tiny with a big grin.

"I did? Yeah, I guess I did at that. But while I was looking for you, you were off having a good time."

"Cyrus told us that there was a time to play. And besides," Tiny continued, sounding quite assertive, "when we were entering the Dark Forest, you told me I would have friends galore. Do you remember saying that?"

"Ah, yeah. I sure do."

"Well, I'm learning it's easy making friends."

"Does that mean you have outgrown your shyness?"

"Oh, no," said Tiny, his dancing eyes doing their thing. "I'm still the shy one, but I'm no longer afraid to take the first step."

"And if someone yells boo, do you hide in your shell?"

"No way! Those days are over," he said with a chuckle, sounding just like Cyrus.

Roberta gave Tiny a double look. "You sure are getting spunky."

"You use to say you liked my spunkiness."

Roberta smiled, "I still do."

"I like it when you have a happy face."

"I'm trying to take life less serious. But it's a constant struggle."

"Have you been talking with Cyrus?" asked Tiny, with a half tilt of his head.

"Not since we were all together. I've searched everywhere but without any luck. Have you seen him?"

"Nope. But I'm sure if he's not here, he's on his way."

"I don't really have any doubts, Tiny. I just wish he would get here and soon. I seem to have developed a bad case of worry."

"Why don't you relax and let Cyrus find you. It would be a lot easier that way."

Ignoring his suggestion, she changed the subject. "By the way, who are your new friends?"

"Oh, I've met a few Lizards and a large family of Snakes."

Roberta could feel the cold shivers go down her spine, but before she had time to react, Tiny laughed. "Have you ever tried to shake hands with a Snake?"

Caught off guard by Tiny's quickness, Roberta stepped back to give him another long look. Then between a quick grin and a shudder she inquired, "Are all your new friends Reptiles?"

"Actually, I did come across an old acquaintance. The Cheetah. And he says to tell you he's trying to change his spots."

"Really!" blurted Roberta with complete amazement.

Tiny glanced up with a very big grin. "Nope. I was just joshing you. Having a little fun."

Roberta slowly shook her head. "You really had me going that time."

"Yep," Tiny replied as they both joined in laughing.

"But Tiny, please don't tease me about that ill-tempered demon. I have enough to worry about as it is. And I do believe you like playing with my mind."

"Not really," he grinned with that childlike innocence. " It just comes out that way. "

Roberta looked at Tiny as though seeing him for the first time. "Tiny, I'm happy that you're making new friends. And I can clearly see that you don't need me to hold your hand. So let's plan to meet at the Grand Assembly for The Elder's presentation. Okay?"

"Okay. I'd like that."

"And if I get there before you, I'll save you a seat. That way we can share this historic day together."

"Sounds good to me," replied Tiny.

"Then I'll see you at high noon. And Tiny, try to be on time." Then almost forgetting, she let loose a big smile. "Oh, when I returned home, I was blessed with four baby brothers and three baby sisters."

"Oh, my! *Eighteen* sisters and brothers," uttered Tiny with a blushing grin. "And thirty-six looong ears to wash. Mercy. Mercy."

Roberta laughed. "You and your numbers. See you at the assembly."

With one of her famous jack-rabbit starts, she sprinted off. Turning on her speed, she again searched high and low, but Cyrus was not to be found.

When Roberta returned to where she had left Tiny, she was in for another surprise. He was nearby, sharing his blueberries with a half dozen Monkeys, who in turn, were sharing their bananas.

Roberta joined them for introductions, but politely declined the fruit, saying she was just too anxious to eat anything. As the introductions were being made, Tiny proceeded to get some of their names confused, but no one gave it a second thought.

Roberta was about to resume her search, when Tiny again suggested that she slow down and relax, saying that Cyrus would arrive at the perfect time.

This time, Roberta gave Tiny a very long look, thinking how much her friend had changed. And as before, she chose not to take his suggestion, and scooted off leaving Tiny with his new troop of playmates.

Roberta decided that this time she was going to check every corner of the park, and with her speed it didn't take her long to reach the other side. There, to her pleasant surprise, she saw an old friend.

From under a shady tree, Herminia Horse had been observing Roberta's erratic behavior. When Roberta stopped to say hello, Herminia advised her to stop hopping about and to follow her example by taking life in stride.

Roberta with a half grin, shook her head. "That may be all right for you, but striding is not my style." After sharing pleasantries, Roberta was about to dash off, when Herminia revealed some news that was devastating.

Roberta's ears went limp. "The Cheetah is here?!" she exclaimed. "And he's looking for me?! It's the Tiger's curse! Thomas, I don't hate you any more!"

Herminia looked baffled. "What did you say? Do you believe in curses?"

"Herminia, forget what I just said. I have so much on my mind, I'm afraid I'm losing it. Now I really must find Cyrus."

"You know he would tell you not to worry."

"Thanks, Herminia, but that's easier said than done. If I'm still here, save a seat for Tiny and me. I gotta run."

"Will do my friend. And please don't worry. You'll get wrinkles under those beautiful blue eyes of yours."

With a hurried goodbye, Rapid Roberta took off with one of her jack-rabbit starts. With increased determination, she zoomed through the park. Her troubled thoughts were equally divided between looking out for the vengeful Beast and searching for Cyrus, now glancing skyward in hopes of finding him.

Now that his tummy was full, Tiny was content just to relax in the warm sunlight. He was also fascinated to see Creatures of every size and breed, from Aardvarks to Zebras.

There were some Creatures, however, that filled Tiny with fear. They were the Gorillas. He was not used to seeing hairy bipeds walking upright on two legs. For Tiny, these monstrous-sized primates looked so different and frightful, especially the ones that weighted six hundred pounds or more. They were awesome.

Scared or not, Tiny had promised himself that on this special day, he would not withdraw into his shell. Besides, by hiding within himself, he would certainly miss some action. And that wouldn't be any fun. But those gigantic Creatures might have to wait another day, even if they do have bananas to share.

Then again, Tiny knew that someday he would need to overcome his fears. Maybe he was ready to meet a muscular Gorilla after all.

At that very moment, turning to his right, Tiny saw a large family of Snakes and Lizards by the rippling stream. He decided to join them for another cool swim, feeling quite comfortable with his distant cousins. But then, that would be too easy.

Deep down inside, Tiny *knew* that if he wanted to continue to grow, he would need to go beyond his comfort zone. "Better stick my neck out and move forward," he said to himself. And he did, even though very slowly.

A short time later, Tiny stopped to take a deep breath. With renewed confidence, he took a big step in the direction of where the giant-sized Gorillas were having their late morning snack of sweet, ripe bananas. Tiny was on his way.

Chapter 34

"Oh, no!" gasped Roberta, her ears thumping frantically. It was the Beast! For a terrifying moment, Roberta was unable to speak or run. This time there would be no escape.

"Good day," greeted the Cheetah, standing in her way. "You're just the one I've been waiting for. Do you recall our last, er, encounter?"

"I'm afraid I do," uttered Roberta, bracing herself for a jack-rabbit start.

"Relax Roberta. You have nothing to fear from me."

"Oh," she replied, not believing one word of it. Thinking only of escape, she was prepared to take off at his first threatening move. But by that time, it could be too late.

The jungle Cat, as was his style, took command. Smoothly, the sleek feline controlled the confrontation. "If you recall, I promised we'd meet again."

"It was a threat," Roberta corrected under her breath. "Something about having my furry hide."

"And since I'm one for keeping my word," the Cheetah continued uninterrupted. "I wanted an opportunity to chat with you."

"To chat? To have my ears on a trophy more than likely," she thought bitterly.

"Since our last, ah, lunch break, I've learned a few things."

"Lunch break?!" Roberta thought with a smirk. "Your lunch and my broken neck."

Not getting a response from Roberta, the spotted Beast continued. "For one thing, I've heard of your proposal to bring about a peaceful jungle."

"You know of my Crusade?" she blurted with mixed feelings, her eyes still locked on the Cheetah's every move.

"Yes I have. And I want you to know, I've decided to support your cause."

For a solitary moment, Roberta stiffened. "You're lying. This is some kind of mean trick of yours."

The slick Cat purred. "Be serious. If I wanted your furry hide, I'd have it by now, tricks notwithstanding."

Still fearful of the Cheetah's motives, Roberta was completely flustered and didn't know what to think. She took an extra deep breath. "I'm overwhelmed. And if you're telling me the truth, I do accept your support."

"You'll be pleased to know that my support also includes all my friends. We'll be there with our vote."

Roberta scratched her furry head. "A moment ago, you were the last one I wanted to see. Now you've given me new hope that my Crusade has a chance."

The Cheetah grinned, showing his sharp fangs. "Not so fast Rapid Roberta. The Elder will have to confront the hostile opposition of a number of clans, including King Lion and Queen Cobra."

"You're right, of course. I'm prone to jump to hasty conclusions." Roberta hesitated, then said, "Besides saying thank you, I don't know what else to say. I'm beyond words."

"No problem," stated the Cheetah, now sounding impatient. "By the time you think of something, I'll be gone. I get restless staying in one spot too long."

"Are you in a hurry?"

"I'm always in a hurry. It's my style."

"You're also quick with the words," said Roberta, feeling less tense, but still keeping out a sharp eye. "Can I tell my friends that you have changed your spots?"

The self-assured Beast flashed a toothy smile. "I wouldn't go as far as that. Just say I've turned over a new leaf." Then, no sooner said, the Cheetah shifted his weight to his powerful hind legs, prepared to spring forward.

"Before you dash off," Roberta cried out, "what's your name and- - - ?"

But before Roberta could complete her thought, the streamlined Cat was on his way like a heated flash. Turning his spotted head, he called back,

"My name is Charlie, but my friends call me Mr. Charles." Now only a yellow blur, he roared, "Good luck, my friend."

The Cheetah was gone, leaving Roberta with thoughts rushing through her head. "This is marvelous. I dare say, my Great Crusade does have a chance. I can't wait to see Tiny's face when I tell him about the big Cat. Why, he'll think I'm joshing him back."

Standing there and trying to be somewhat rational, a sense of gratitude filled her senses. She was about to say that she was sooome Rabbit, but for some unknown reason, it no longer seemed appropriate. In fact, she couldn't remember the last time she needed to say it.

Following a quiet moment, that *deep down feeling* was all consuming. Looking skyward, Roberta gave thanks to where she knew it rightfully belonged. "Thank you, Great Spirit. And Cyrus, I know you had a part in this, one way or another."

Roberta thought for a moment, then went on to say, "And just to play it safe, although I feel a little foolish, I'll thank you, too, Sir Thomas." Then with a chuckle, she added, "I really don't believe in curses. Tiny knows that."

"What a marvelous day this has been," reflected Roberta. "First, my new circle of friends, and now to have the support of Mr. Charles. What could possibly happen next?"

After another moment of gratitude, she headed back to find her friend. "Tiny should have been here with me," she thought. "Well, it's his loss. He's probably with those cute little Monkeys," she added with a loud laugh. "What a day this has been. Tiny, where are you?"

A winged shadow crossed her path. She quickly glanced upward. And there he was, flying high above the crowd. "Tiny was right," thought a much relieved Roberta. "Cyrus has arrived at the perfect time."

From above, Cyrus saw Roberta waving excitedly, and he responded with a dip of his wing.

Roberta was overjoyed and began to hop and skip about, beyond caring how she might appear to others. And to some, she looked downright foolish.

Following a gliding descent, they shared a warm embrace. "Lovely to see you, my dear Roberta."

"I knew you would be on time!" she exclaimed, forgetting all about the needless worry she had put herself through. "How was your flight?"

Cyrus was about to respond but he never had a chance. Roberta, forgetting all about decorum, was now talking much faster than usual. He didn't seem to mind as he listened intently to all that she had to share, including Tiny and the Monkeys, her encounter with Mr. Charles, and the new arrival of her baby sisters and brothers.

"That's wonderful," Cyrus squeezed in when Roberta paused briefly to catch her breath. "You and your parents must be very proud indeed."

"Oh, my yes, they are! I mean, we are! Oh, you know what I mean. Anyway, my Mom and Pop are here, and I told them all about you - - - and they very much want to meet you - - - and, and they all love to hug!"

Cyrus laughed heartily, his head bobbing. "I'm looking forward to meeting your parents and siblings, hugs and all."

"Oh, it's so wonderful to see you again. So much has happened the last few days. And wait until you see Tiny. He's outgrown his need to pout and he has changed so much I'm having a hard time keeping up with him."

"Is that one of your exaggerations?" said Cyrus with a boyish grin. Not waiting for a response, he continued. "It will bring joy to these old eyes to see Tiny again, and to meet his new Monkey friends."

"His new friends also include Lizards and Snakes," she said with an obvious quiver.

"Wonderful! I'm sure I would enjoy meeting all of Tiny's friends."

Roberta's long ears twitched. "I'm not so sure I can go that far, but I'm trying. Really!"

Cyrus gently touched her with the tip of his wing. "I can see that you are. And maybe more than you realize."

At that moment, Roberta remembered to tell Cyrus about CeZar and their successful rebellion against Queen Cobra. Having done that, she then asked Cyrus a question that she just couldn't shake free.

There was that serious look in her eye. "Cyrus, did you have anything to do with Mr. Charles changing his mind about me and my Crusade?"

Without hesitation, Cyrus replied, "Roberta, the answer to your question is no."

"Then how did you know?"

"Roberta, I didn't have any knowledge of what the Cheetah might do. What I did know was that no one can run away from their problems. To have excluded Mr. Charles would be like running away. One finds solutions by going through the apparent problem, not by avoidance."

Roberta slowly nodded her head. "To find solutions, I must go forward and I was going backwards."

Cyrus reached over and gave her a reassuring caress. "We can learn by looking back. But living backwards causes only torment and a new set of problems, usually self-inflicted."

Roberta became unusually quiet, trying to think it through. Cyrus chose to move on. "It's my desire that as soon as possible that the three of us get together. It will be a joy to see Tiny again. I never knew that seven days could seem so long."

"Me, too," shared Roberta. "Were you lonely? I was."

Cyrus smiled, "No, Roberta. Alone but not lonely. Nature does not adhere to a vacuum, and there were preparations for today's activities that needed attending."

"Did you see The Elder?" she asked, with increasing anticipation.

"Yes, indeed. And it was most rewarding and entertaining, far beyond my words to express."

"The Elder must be someone very special."

"Let's just say that in spiritual awareness, The Elder is beyond compare as you and the Grand Assembly will soon see."

"It's still awfully hard for me to believe that there is someone more worthy than you."

Cyrus slowly nodded. "Much of what I am today is due to my continued friendship with The Elder. And it is my pleasure to tell you that The Elder shares your excitement, knowing that today's proceedings are due largely to your courage and vision."

Feeling uneasy, Roberta blushed. "Thank you, Cyrus. I guess I just don't like being someone's lunch. Living in constant danger is no way to live."

"Many seem to agree with you. And because you took the first step, our kingdom may someday regain our lost paradise."

It was obvious that Roberta was still feeling self-conscious, so Cyrus diverted the attention elsewhere. "Roberta, you and Tiny did your part, now it's time for The Elder to take the next step."

"Cyrus," she said pensively, "is The Elder more powerful than King Lion?"

Cyrus thought for a moment, searching for a few words to best answer a complex question. "The Elder's power is beyond physical power. It's the power of Love."

Roberta lowered her head, appearing confused. "I think you answered my question, but I don't fully understand."

"Knowing that you don't know is a good start. When you allow yourself to see with your heart, you will understand." After a brief pause: "For the heart has eyes the mind knows not."

Roberta slowly shuck her head. "Cyrus, after The Elder's presentation, do you think the Grand Assembly will accept my proposal?"

"Roberta," he said with a broad smile, "I guess it bears repeating. I fly in the sky I occupy. The future will be here soon enough."

"In other words, stay in the here and now."

"And to be responsible for your own choices," confirmed Cyrus. "And The Elder will do the same. Then, whatever the Grand Assembly decides to do, the lesson of *acceptance* will be upon us."

Cyrus glanced skyward. "Roberta, it's time for me to leave."

Roberta hesitated for a moment, then said softly, "Before you go, I need a big hug. I'm starting to feel fearful of what might happen if my Crusade is defeated."

Choosing to ignore her fears, Cyrus responded only to her request. With a warm gleam in his eye, he smiled. "There's always time for one more hug."

Following their heartfelt embrace, Cyrus took to the air, leaving Roberta with her dream and her fears.

Chapter 35

Cyrus completed his final preparations. With the bright sun nearing its apex, the introduction of The Elder was near.

Symbolic of unity, the outdoor auditorium was arranged in the round. The tiered redwood seats gave everyone a clear view of the circular stage below.

High above the ancient evergreens that surrounded the amphitheater, a few white clouds drifted serenely across the light blue sky. Off in the distance, the ageless, purple mountains could be seen. A gentle breeze off the nearby sea cooled the jungle's heat as it swept through the multicolored leaves.

One member of the Grand Assembly squirmed nervously in her seat. Concerned with hopes and fears, Roberta was again up on her feet.

"Try to relax." The advice came from Herminia Horse who was sitting to Roberta's right.

"I wish I could. But I'm worried about Tiny. He should be here by now. And what if my proposal is defeated? More violence, I fear." Trying to fight back her frustration, Roberta turned again to scan the oval stadium. "Tiny, where are you? I knew I should have stayed with him."

"Roberta, if you would slow down a bit. I've been trying to tell you that Tiny was seen with a band of Gorillas."

"Total nonsense!" she blurted. "Monkeys or Reptiles, but not Gorillas!"

Herminia flipped her dark brown mane. "That's what I heard."

"He has to be here," asserted Roberta. Standing on her toes, she searched every which way. But Tiny was not to be seen.

In the very top row, she happened to see Edi and her circle of friends. After they greeted each other with a hearty wave, Roberta swung her attention back to finding Tiny. Further down she saw Mr. Charles. He appeared to be in a deep discussion with several Tigers and Leopards. Odd, she thought, there were no Lions in his group.

"Oh, no!" grimaced Roberta. "The sight of him turns my stomach."

"Who are you referring to?" asked Herminia.

"Head-in-the-Sand Osbert Ostrich. He's so passive, living without purpose. He makes me sick."

"I would never give anyone that kind of power over me. Besides, look again and see who has his attention."

"Why, it's Glenn Giraffe."

"If anyone can get Osbert to make a commitment, it's gentleman Glenn. It might not be easy, but Glenn is both patient and quietly persuasive."

Roberta nodded, then resumed her search for Tiny. "Oh, oh." Roberta began to shudder. "Won't I ever be able to see a snake without quivering?" Across the way sat the Cobras that had broken away from the Queen.

"CeZar is doing his part," thought Roberta. She had heard that CeZar was the leader of the rebels, and that their numbers were growing. But her optimism was short lived. In the first three rows, completely surrounding the circular stage, were the hostile Cobras. An alarmed Roberta spotted Queen Cobra. With her cold, sinister grin, the Queen sat coiled in the front row, protected by her loyal guards.

"She's out to terrify The Elder," surmised Roberta. "I knew she was up to no good."

Herminia agreed. "I know from *personal experiences,* Cobras can strike at any time, and when you least expect it."

"Now what?!" exclaimed Roberta. Coming down the aisle to her left was a Creature who was causing quite a commotion. Before Roberta had a chance to react, the Creature flopped in the seat next to a startled Roberta. "I was saving - - -"

"Thanks," interrupted the rude intruder. "I'll take it. When I'm done with it, you can have it back. If you find any quills, you may keep them as a souvenir of Pruddy Porcupine. And your name?"

A flustered Roberta pulled back her head and replied faintly, "I'm Roberta."

"Oh, you're the one," said the Porcupine, sounding not at all impressed.

"Don't argue with her," advised Herminia. Then, trying to make light of it, she suggested, "And this is not one of those times for your famous rabbit punch."

"What should I do?" asked Roberta, still unnerved.

With a straight face, she replied, "Use good Horse sense." Then adding quickly, "Better yet, send love."

"What if she doesn't want it?"

"Send it anyway."

Before Roberta could respond, the brash Porcupine was saying, "I see the Cobras have taken the front rows."

"To intimidate The Elder," Roberta replied brusquely.

"Your ignorance precedes your mouth," declared the Porcupine. "The Cobras are nearsighted. Everyone knows that. But then again, Queen Cobra does have a reputation for being treacherous. We'll just have to wait and see."

Not waiting for a response, the Porcupine turned to the stage. "It's about that time. Let's get this show started."

Roberta looked skyward. It was high noon. The capacity crowd stirred with anticipation, and those just arriving hurried to find a seat. But her little friend was not among them. With or without Tiny, the Grand Assembly was about to begin. "Tiny, where are you? I pray that you're all right."

Even though her concern for Tiny was deep, a sense of joy rushed through Roberta when she saw a familiar figure making his way across the outdoor stage. An anxious hush came over the congregation.

Cyrus the Great Horned Owl, composed and dignified, made his announcement in a clear, vibrant voice. "Welcome to the Grand Assembly. It is my distinguished honor to present Zoe Theodosia, The Elder."

Right on cue, a troop of three White-headed Monkeys and a Turtle carried in a circular enclosure. With pinpoint precision, they placed the enclosure at center stage. Together, they promptly left the stage to take their seats. (No it wasn't Tiny.)

A curtain of leaves and flowers completely covered the enclosure. Its beauty was enhanced by its simplicity. No more than three feet high, it rested on four small legs. Without any delay, the curtain parted, and there for all to see - - -

Roberta rose up from her seat, bringing her paws to her flushed face. She was stunned with disbelief. That many appeared to share her reaction was evident by the constant murmur that rippled through the crowd.

At that moment, Roberta's fear of defeat was greater than her hope. She slumped back into her seat. "She's only half my size. And Cyrus told me she had power. I don't see it. My Crusade is over before it's had a chance to begin."

"Now don't go jumping to conclusions" consoled Herminia. "We need to give The Elder her chance."

"That little lady could have a million chances and she would still face defeat," countered the Porcupine. " She appears too fragile if you ask me. I don't think she has what it takes."

Ignoring the crude intruder, Roberta's ears began to quiver. Hissing came from the Cobras who were seating nearest the stage. Over to her far left, several giant-sized Gorillas jeered, while the Tigers roared with catcalls.

To show respect, a majority of the members stood and applauded. Edi and her friends, with undaunted loyalty, led the way. When the applause died down, a disturbing undertone pulsated through the Grand Assembly.

The crowd's obvious apprehension was greeted by a warm, gentle smile. A few unkind remarks about her size were heard, but that did not seem to disturb the calm confidence of the Earth Worm.

"Thank you, Cyrus, my dear friend. It's always a deep joy to see you." Cyrus acknowledged The Elder with a courteous bow, then took his seat off stage.

An uneasy stillness befell the congregation. The only movement came from center stage, where the Earth Worm turned slowly around, her soft eyes comprising the community.

Then, in a voice surprisingly full, the Earth Worm began. "It's my devoted pleasure to welcome you to the Grand Assembly. I express my gratitude to one and all for making the commitment to be here. Although there is little that I can do for you, there is much we can do for each other."

The Elder paused. "Before I continue to present the proposal at hand, our Great Spirit wants you to know that each one of you are dearly Loved."

Many lowered their heads. It was obvious that they were deeply moved by what they had heard.

For some unexplained reason, which Roberta did not understand at the time, The Elder appeared to be both vulnerable and yet, to be in complete control of her presence.

The Earth Worm brought her hands to her lips and bowed reverently. After a moment of silence, she raised her head. "Now let us begin. We are here today for the purpose to consider a proposal that would change the very nature of our way of life. I am honored to be your servant on this noble endeavor."

The Porcupine agreed and whispered, "I'd rather have a servant than a master any day."

The Elder continued. "One of my teachers had a grand vision. This vision centered with the hope of casting a great shadow that would touch many future generations."

The Earth Worm paused to extend her small body to her fullest height. Slowly turning, she extended her hands over her head. With a playful smile she said, "Even when stretched to the limit, I am all of fifteen inches tall. You can clearly see that there is no way I can cast such a shadow. Even at sundown, my shadow would not cross this stage, let alone several generations."

A scattering of light and uneven laughter was heard, which prompted the Earth Worm to give a casual nod. Then, with a generous smile, she said, "Now, if I had the graceful body of Glenn Giraffe, without a doubt, my shadow would be quite impressive."

More laughter greeted The Elder who again nodded politely.

On the far side of the theater, sitting between two powerfully built Gorillas, Tiny thought to himself, "I wonder how much Zoe weighs?"

"For those who are curious," the Earth Worm offered warmly, "I weigh nearly twelve pounds when soaking wet."

The assemblage responded with sporadic laughter and a brief but louder applause with Tiny leading the way.

Roberta turned to her left and by chance spotted Tiny. She almost fell out of her seat. "Herminia, there's Tiny sitting with all those Gorillas. I'm flabbergasted! Do you think he'll be all right?"

Herminia smiled. "You sound like a worried mother. Tiny is growing up. Let him be."

Roberta's troubled thoughts were interrupted when she heard the softly spoken words from the stage. "There is little anyone can do alone. But if we plan and work together, side by side, we could emit a shadow so grand that it would travel across many generations."

This brought a few snickering remarks from the Gorillas. They strongly believed that they were big enough to take care of themselves and had no need to join with others. To show off their mighty size, four of the largest Gorillas jumped to their feet and uttered several more cutting remarks about The Elder's size.

Roberta was incensed. "Herminia, those Gorillas are terribly rude and their insults are totally uncalled for."

"Yes, my dear, but getting upset won't help you or The Elder."

"Shhh," admonished the Porcupine, "*Your* little lady is confronting those oversized Gorillas."

Roberta, still angry, looked up to see that the Earth Worm had turned to face the taunting Gorillas. Zoe's gentle expression never wavered. "Thank you for expressing your point of view. That is why we are here. With open dialogue we can better understand one another. And what you say about *your* size is true. You have good reason to be proud."

Still facing the Gorillas, the Earth Worm continued without a trace of anger. "Consider how your size and vitality would benefit all of us. Your super strength is essential for our monumental quest. With your loyal support, we could build a better world for everyone. It is my hope that you choose to join us."

Tiny, who nodded with gusto, gave a burly Gorilla a good-natured poke. The four standing Gorillas looked at each other, then back to the Earth Worm. Then, one by one sat down, choosing to keep their remarks to themselves.

The Porcupine leaned over to Roberta and said, "I would never dare confront a Gorilla, but they are really a docile lot. But what will happen when *your* little lady is challenged by King Lion or Queen Cobra? I do believe that a confrontation with those two tyrants can't be avoided."

Roberta found that thought quite disturbing, but said nothing. She was also feeling a growing admiration for The Elder.

Zoe turned to encompass the community. "Regardless of one's size, be it grand or small, there is little anyone can do alone. But if each of us would contribute that which we do best, then our chance of success is enhanced that much more."

Spontaneous applause encircled the auditorium.

The Elder raised her hand to show her appreciation. "If I may digress for just a moment and say that as long as *my* small but solid body continues to be long enough to touch the ground, than I am *perfectly suited* for me."

Random laughter broke free, followed by more applause, while several muscular Gorillas shifted in their seats embarrassed.

Roberta looked about and sensed less tension in the air. She released a heavy sigh and turned to Herminia, who gave her a reassuring smile.

Facing the large audience, the Earth Worm continued. "In a deeper sense, size is secondary. One's real strength comes from within."

There followed a deliberate pause. Again slowly turning she continued. "We have forgotten the ways of our forefathers. Somewhere, long ago, we stumbled off our path and lost our way. And for that we have suffered much. Suffering that was unnecessary and unwanted.

"There was a time when our forefathers lived in peace and harmony. When the Lion and the Lamb shared the same meadow without fear and the Vipers had no need of their poisonous fangs.

"Our Great Spirit provided our forefathers with all of their needs and did so abundantly. Our kingdom was a paradise, and our forefathers enjoyed a life of contentment and Love. Today, we struggle with violence and hate."

As Zoe slowly turned, her voice was free of bitterness and resentment. "What happened long ago happened. The past is over. We can choose to release all judgment and blame. Today, we have an opportunity to find a solution that will allow each one of us to enjoy a better tomorrow."

A general applause greeted The Elder, who raised, then lowered her left hand to acknowledge her gratitude.

Composed, Zoe contemplated her next approach. For what was required was certain to bring strong and bitter opposition. Some might even contend that what she was about to say was offensive, though none was intended.

The Elder was prepared to encounter King Lion. "There are some of us who have chosen to live by the law of tooth and claw. Those who remember the past know that physical power is self-destructive. And for those who choose to live by the claw will die by the claw."

Without a moment lost, the majestic King Lion roared his defiance, his fangs glistening in the sunlight. "The kingdom belongs to those who have the power," he roared again. "And no puny Earth Worm can change that!"

Raucous laughter consumed the coliseum.

With the snap of his claws, the King's Golden Horde jumped to their feet and roared as one united force. The crescendo ROCKED the arena.

A terrified Roberta raised her paws to cover her ears. When the mighty roar subsided, she turned to Herminia. "Now the Lions are threatening her! Why are they so vicious!?"

"It goes with her responsibilities," said Herminia, maintaining a measure of calm. "Remember, she is The Elder."

"I know," uttered Roberta, slowly shaking her head. "But she looks so helpless."

"In her eyes," reassured Herminia, " I see invincibility. Being defenseless is not the same as being helpless."

"When the Lions roared," observed the Porcupine, "*your* little lady didn't even flinch. She's either hard of hearing or very brave."

King Lion, having made his point, gave a second command and his obedient subjects took their seats in unison with an ear shattering THUD.

"Awesome!" came the Porcupine.

A disturbing murmur swept through the crowd. An outbreak of violence was feared by many.

When the Lions roared, The Elder had quietly waited for the opportunity to respond. Now was that time. With decorum and humility, the Earth Worm confronted the King. "When I speak of raw power causing our self-destruction, I mean you nor your royal pride any dishonor. You and I know, where there is Love there is no need of power."

A loud applause rushed through the coliseum. The Lions and the Cobras, however, displayed their united opposition by remaining resolute.

King Lion maintained his steady glare. A low, menacing growl could be heard from his clinched jaws. The King's feline Beasts followed his lead, and their united growl vibrated throughout the arena.

Greatly alarmed, Roberta raised up from her seat. "How can The Elder escape the King's anger? I would willingly give up my Crusade to spare her any harm."

"Despair is of no value," consoled Herminia. "What she needs is our prayers'"

"And a thousands body guards wouldn't hurt," suggested the Porcupine.

Roberta, her eyes fixed on The Elder, thought aloud, "Where is her power that Cyrus talked about? I still don't see it."

Zoe, her soft eyes still centered on the King, moved closer to her counterpart. "King Lion, our violent past reveals that raw power is unreal and fleeting, while Love is real and everlasting. With your benign leadership and keen awareness, you and I know that when we examine our past, we come to realize that physical power leads ultimately to self-destruction. To survive all we need is Love."

A large majority of the Grand Assembly stood and applauded their approval. The Elder raised her right hand to acknowledge their support.

Not to be outperformed by the Earth Worm, King Lion narrowed his large, yellow eyes and glared. But to his surprise, he was greeted with a cordial smile.

Zoe paused, and her soft eyes bonded with the glaring eyes of King Lion. "Today we have the opportunity to join together for the very survival of our kingdom. You and I know that on one level your power seems real. But on a *higher level*, the only power that is real is the power of Love."

There followed an anxious hush over the arena. All eyes shifted from center stage to King Lion, then back to the Earth Worm.

Suddenly, King Lion rose to his feet. With a flick of his golden mane, his disciplined subjects stood erect. Then to the astonishment of the Grand Assembly, the King gave The Elder an exalted bow, which was quickly followed in precise unison by his loyal clan.

While Roberta stared in disbelief, The Elder acknowledged King Lion with a gracious, deep bow.

King Lion, with his powerful paw, gave the Earth Worm a casual salute. A command was given with a swish of his tail, and the King's Golden Horde took their seats with a solid THUD that again ROCKED the coliseum.

"I'm beyond amazement," uttered Roberta, her voice just above a whisper. "First The Elder subdued the Gorillas, and now she has King Lion giving her the respect she fully deserves."

"Your optimism is always pleasing to my ear," said Herminia. "Despair is always a heavy load to bear."

"Well, a salute is not a vote," interjected the Porcupine. "I will say, though, *your* little lady has courage. But will she be able to stand up to the cold-hearted Queen Cobra and her loyal guards? I think not. There's a reason she is known as the Mean Queen."

That alone caused Roberta's body to shudder. Trying to ignore the Porcupine, Roberta returned her attention back to the circular stage.

The Earth Worm again turning to face the audience, continued. "To forsake physical power is to give up nothing, for it is nothing more than a fleeting illusion. But do we have the wisdom to turn away from the path of darkness and the courage to face the light of a new day?"

Enraged, Queen Cobra raised her hooded head. Her cold eyes locked tight on her Jungle adversary. But the Queen's deadly stare was greeted with a warm smile. There was no fear or hate in Zoe's eyes, only Love, but the Queen failed to see it.

Queen Cobra coiled her long, sleek body prepared to strike. "I have no need of light," she hissed with contempt. "And I have no fear of darkness or of you!"

Before the Earth Worm could respond, the Queen flicked the tip of her tail, and her loyal guards raised their hooded heads above the stage.

Roberta shuddered, rushing her paws to her face. "I knew Queen Cobra couldn't be trusted!"

Herminia agreed. "With Cobras you have to watch your every step."

"If the little lady stays clear of the first row of Cobras," offered Pruddy, "she should be safe from any immediate danger."

"If," uttered a deeply fearful Roberta.

Then to the assembly's amazement, Zoe, surrounded by hissing Cobras, moved toward the Queen.

Queen Cobra remained coiled in her seat. Her deadly stare never left its mark.

When only three feet from the Queen, the Earth Worm stopped. The softness in Zoe's eyes revealed her steadfast compassion. She brought her hands together below her chin as though in prayer.

With the hissing in Roberta's ears, Zoe addressed the Queen. "For those who have not overcome the tight grip of fear, you can be our teacher.

Today, we seek those who have the courage to leave the pit of darkness and embrace the light."

The coiled Queen was now swaying from side to side. Her cold stare remained constant. "I have too many enemies to change now," she hissed.

The Earth Worm replied, her voice kind and reassuring, "The best thing we can do with an enemy is to accept him or her as a friend."

Queen Cobra, with her darting tongue, hissed, "I have too many out there who hate me. How do I get *them* to change?"

"By your example. But your responsibility is not to change others. You are here to change only *you.* And to make the first move to be a friend takes the highest form of courage. Friendship starts with tolerance and is followed by respect, then trust. As we continue to grow, eventually we reach the highest level of friendship. It's the level of Love."

"Love," responded the Queen. "I know the word. I do love my family."

Zoe smiled. "I hear and see your Love, my friend. And for those who fail to see the Love that is here and all around us, all you need do is pray for better eyesight."

Light, spontaneous laughter from a very few reached the stage. The Elder quietly acknowledged their understanding.

Queen Cobra, still swaying, was in no mood for laughter. But there in her eyes, the Earth Worm saw a growing softness.

Silently, her intentions still unknown, the Mean Queen raised her head high above the stage, now only inches away from her rival.

The Earth Warm, composed, stood perfectly still waiting for Queen Cobra to respond. Except for the constant hissing, an anxious silence surrounded the coliseum.

Herminia let go a deep sigh. "The Elder's courage is far beyond anything I could have imagined. Of that I have no doubt".

Pruddy sharply disagreed. "Courage or ignorance, your little lady has met her counterpart. The Earth Worm is doomed to fail."

Roberta, prone to argue, flicked her long ears, but kept her disturbing thoughts to herself: "Why does The Elder put herself in danger? My Crusade is not worth her life."

There was a loud horrific gasp from the crowd. From the far side of the stage, a score of Cobras began to slither toward the Earth Worm, then stopped abruptly with the Queen's sharp command. All eyes now focused on the Queen and The Elder.

Still swaying, the Mean Queen lisped, "Zoe - - -" She hesitated. Then after a long delay, her cold stare still fixed on her adversary, hissed, "I want to trust you, and a world without violence does sound tempting."

With a soft smile, the Earth Worm replied, "Queen Cobra, you have taken your first step of friendship. Together, you and I can build a relationship with respect and trust. With your growing awareness, take the Love you have for your family and begin to share it with others, for we are *all one family,* created by our Great Spirit."

Queen Cobra, no longer swaying, lowered her hooded head. It was evident that the Queen was deeply moved by Zoe's words.

"Cyrus was right," thought Roberta. "The Earth Worm does have power."

Herminia was beyond words. With her eyes closed, she slowly bowed her head.

Pruddy touched Roberta's arm and said, "I do believe there are tears in her eyes."

"Whose eyes?" Roberta asked hurriedly, turning back to the stage.

"Why, Queen Cobra's," answered Pruddy. "And I was to believe she had a heart of evil, frozen in stone."

Herminia opened her eyes. "There is nothing more poisonous than rumors filled with hate and prejudice."

A tranquil hush encircled the stage. The Queen and Zoe shared a quiet interlude. At some point during their encounter, the hissing of her loyal subjects had stopped. At what moment in time, no one could remember. Now, simultaneously, Zoe and the Queen bowed, manifesting their mutual respect and trust.

The Earth Worm returned to center stage, while Queen Cobra again bowed her hooded head. On command, her obedient subjects bowed in unison, then slid back into their seats without a sound disturbing the midday air.

"The crisis seems to be over," Roberta said with a heavy sigh.

"The power of prayer can never be overvalued," offered Herminia.

"She's amazing," observed Pruddy. "I'm totally, but pleasantly surprised. I wonder if there are others who plan to challenge *our* little lady."

Roberta turned to give the Porcupine a hard, dubious stare. But then simply replied, “I hope not. I don’t think I can take any more.”

The Earth Worm, with her gentle presence, was prepared for the next encounter. “Is there anyone who would like to express their point of view?”

A long silence followed. Many started to glance about. The Elder looked out among the capacity crowd. “This is no time to be shy,” she smiled. “As you can see, I’m completely harmless.”

A scattering of easy laughter moved through the oval theater. Tiny let loose a big grin saying to himself, “That’s me. The shy one.”

Silence again reclaimed the community. Turning slowly, Zoe patiently waited. She wanted to make sure that ample time was allowed if someone might want to speak out. And then, someone did.

“On behave of the Grand Assembly,” said a vibrant voice from the last row, “I want to express our gratitude from us to you. With a full heart, we thank you.”

With a disarming smile, Zoe replied, “One never grows too old to hear those two beautiful words. Thank you, Edi.”

There followed another long pause. When it seemed obvious that there were to be no immediate challenges, the Earth Worm continued. “There is no way we can change yesterday or remove all the pain we have inflicted on ourselves. But by taking our first step today, we can create a tomorrow free of violence and starvation.”

For Tiny, that last remark brought a look of pure satisfaction as his little eyes did their dance.

Now slowly turning, The Elder continued. “Our Great Spirit bestowed upon us a number of gifts. The greatest of these is Love. By accepting the ultimate gift of Love, we can overcome that which causes our sorrow: Ignorance, fear, greed, and hate.

“What Love creates, lasts forever. And with the force of Love, we can create a legacy for our children and our children’s children that will enable them to live in a world where they will be proud to be who they are.”

Roberta blinked. There was a soft, blue light over Zoe’s head and shoulders. Roberta blinked a second time and the soft light was gone. Or was it just an illusion; or something beyond her awareness?

After a brief pause, the Earth Worm continued. “When we were given the miracle of life, our Great Spirit, at the same time, gave us the gift of free will.

"Today, with that gift, it is you who will decide which path we are to follow. Shall it be the path that leads to our self-destruction? Or shall we choose the path that will allow the gift of life to be equally shared by all? Together, united as one, we can create a new world of peace and compassion.

"As you make your choice for you and your children, remember: Where there is Love, there is no need of power."

A deep calmness embodied the Grand Assembly. It was evident that many were moved by the eloquence of her presentation.

"*We, you and I,* are living in a glorious but precarious time. For we have the power to recreate our lost paradise or the power to destroy everything we hold dear.

"My dear friends, your future lies with *you* . Look into your hearts, for there *you will* find the path you are to follow."

Still turning, Zoe's soft eyes embraced the whole congregation. "With your acceptance, the last words expressed will be those of our Great Spirit.

The Earth Worm stood perfectly still. At center stage, she bowed her head. With deep reverence, she proclaimed:

"Let Your Choice Today And Forevermore Be Given
With Love And Not For Love. For You Are All Loved Beyond Measure."

The Earth Worm held her hands together as though in prayer. Following a series of gracious bows, Cyrus crossed the stage to join her. Together, they would wait for the Grand Assembly's decision. Their vote was near at hand.

Chapter 36

Roberta sat quietly with her thoughts. She now realized that the gift of free will was not hers alone. It was a gift given equally to everyone. But the greatest gift of all is love. And no matter how the Grand Assembly should vote, Roberta knew she would always have her love to share with others.

Roberta for the first time, could now appreciate the words of Cyrus, when he shared that we need to see with our hearts. She also realized that her crusade was only a fleeting idea, while love was real and forever.

Roberta took a deep breath. She turned to gaze at the purple mountains and far beyond. Releasing her *need* for her crusade, Roberta was overcome by pure joy.

Deep in the heart of the Jungle Kingdom, the stillness was embraced with a thunderous cheer. The Elder's question was answered. Standing as one, the Grand Assembly made its decision: A commitment to create a kingdom for all to live together in peace.

Filled with new hope, the multitude moved towards the center. Mr. Charles lifted Roberta to the stage, followed by Herminia and Pruddy. Already on stage was Tiny, who was riding high on the shoulders of a husky Gorilla.

Roberta and Tiny greeted one another. And at the same moment, they both *felt a deep inner need* to meet others. Tiny directed the Gorilla to find Mr. Charles and Pauline Black Panther, while Roberta found herself with a slither of Cobras. To her pleasant surprise, she had no need to shudder. Well, except for a few mild tremors felt on the tips of her long ears.

Glenn Giraffe, with Osbert, gave Roberta a wink and a smile, then quietly moved on. Roberta, not knowing what had transpired earlier, could only marvel and wonder.

Those who couldn't reach the now overflowing stage, began to dance in the aisles. From Aardvarks to Cobras to Lions to Zebras, all fear and separation were gone. United in spirit, they all moved in and out of small groups. Those who could took each other by the hand to form a spiral-shaped circle. Then by turning and twisting, new spiral-shaped circles were formed, one inside the other.

Over the joyous celebration, The Elder's voice was heard: "With your heartfelt commitment, our grand endeavor to reclaim our lost paradise begins today."

Cyrus was also deeply moved. "As with life, our grand circle has no beginning or ending. But our circle does have a center. And *we* are all IT!"

Then as though one voice, Zoe and Cyrus, lifted up their heads and called out, "Thank you, so much!"

The multitude, now a sea of faces, raised its voice and sang out, "Thank you, so much!"

Their challenge begins anew. If their united endeavor should fail, there is little to fear that their children will survive to blame them. If they fulfill their common cause, their children of future generations will remember and Love them forever.

Tiny and Roberta, now hand-in-hand, remembered that day when they took a chance to reach out and touch. "Tiny, I will always be your friend. Always."

Tiny, with an endearing smile, replied in kind. Then, together they shared their moment with a warm embrace. Following another quiet moment, Roberta looked skyward. Taking liberties with the words of Cyrus, knowing that he wouldn't mind, she softly said:

"I
Pray that our
endeavor has no ending
but only an everlasting Beginning. . . ."

To be continued . . .